PEN P
BOOK FIFTEEN

THE
HEARTBREAK
GUY

by Sharon Dennis Wyeth

A YEARLING BOOK

Published by
Dell Publishing
a division of
Bantam Doubleday Dell Publishing Group, Inc.
666 Fifth Avenue
New York, New York 10103

The trademark Yearling ® is registered in the U.S. Patent and Trademark Office.
The trademark Dell® is registered in the U.S. Patent and Trademark Office.
ISBN: 0-440-40412-6

Illustrations by Wendy Wax
Published by arrangement with Parachute Press, Inc.
Printed in the United States of America
February 1991
10 9 8 7 6 5 4 3 2 1
OPM

For Gary Dennis, Jr.

CHAPTER ONE

Palmer Durand stared out the window, oblivious to the gray and windy day outside and absentmindedly twisting her long blond hair around her finger. Then, with a soft smile, she began to draw hearts in her French notebook. She wrote the initials S.O'L. and P.S.D. in the hearts, humming slightly off-key. As she drew, the hearts became bigger and her humming louder.

"Palmer!" Shanon Davis called from the loveseat.

"What is it?" Palmer asked, her beautiful blue eyes still dreamy as she wrote and rewrote her initials next to S.O'L.

"I can't think with all that humming," Shanon explained, her hazel eyes troubled. She rarely voiced any complaints, for she preferred peace in the suite. "I'm having problems with my English paper."

"You always do great in English," Max Schloss said from behind the Brighton newspaper she was reading.

Shanon, Palmer, and Max were in their sitting room in Fox Hall at the Alma Stephens School for Girls, a private boarding school. Shanon and Max shared a bedroom, and

1

Palmer shared her bedroom with Amy Ho. Max was new to the suite this year because Lisa, Shanon's original roommate, had decided to stay home and live with her mother who had recently separated from her father.

Max was wearing her favorite comfortable clothes—a raspberry-colored sweatshirt and lime-green leggings with thick turquoise socks. Shanon grinned at her roommate; no matter how outrageous her clothes were, they never seemed to clash with her bright red hair. But Shanon's grin disappeared when she looked back down at her blank sheet of paper.

"I'm sorry to be such a drag," she said, "but that paper on *Lord of the Flies* is due Friday. We have to write about the boy we feel is most like us, and I just don't know what to say—I hated all the boys. I hated the whole book!"

"Shanon, you don't have to like a book to do the homework; I never do," Palmer advised as she put an arrow through the biggest heart. "Just do the work and don't think about it."

"Who did you pick, Max?" Shanon asked, ignoring Palmer's comment.

"Piggy."

"Piggy? Why would you want to be him?"

"I don't want to be him, but I sometimes feel like him," Max answered, embarrassed.

"I just don't—" Shanon didn't get a chance to finish her sentence. She was interrupted by the slamming of the door as Amy Ho, their fourth suitemate, walked in. Amy looked upset. Her cheeks were bright red and her black punky hair was more spiked than ever. Dressed in all black except for her red cowboy boots, Amy stormed into the room, flinging off her gloves and coat.

2

"That's it! I'm out of here! This is not the place for me!" Amy announced.

Shanon stood up and walked over to her friend. "What's the matter?" she asked.

"Nobody understands me!" Amy growled.

"Come on, we're the Foxes. You can tell us," Shanon pleaded, putting her arm around Amy.

At the beginning of their first year at Alma, the four original suitemates had advertised for pen pals from Ardsley, the nearby boys' school. In the ad the girls had dubbed themselves "Foxes of the Third Dimension," and the name had stuck. Now that Lisa was gone, Max was a full-fledged member of the group.

Max put down her newspaper. "Spit it out, Amy," she said. "You'll have to get it off your chest sooner or later."

Amy frowned. "It's Kringle!"

"Your voice teacher?" said Shanon. "I thought you liked Professor Bernard, and the fact that he looks like Santa Claus is an added plus!"

"I do," Amy conceded, "but he never lets me do anything I want. He tells me my voice is improving, but all he lets me sing during the lesson are songs that he likes. I mean, how many times can I sing 'Oklahoma'?"

Shanon giggled. Amy was the ultimate New Yorker and "Oklahoma" was definitely not her style.

"It can't be all that bad," she said.

"All I wanted to do was sing a rock song—like a Madonna song—and he wouldn't let me!" Amy complained, plopping herself down in Shanon's abandoned chair.

"Maybe he's worried it would ruin your voice," Max chimed in. "You know, you have to be in control of your voice in order not to hurt it."

3

"That isn't it!" Amy exclaimed, jumping out of the chair, unable to keep still. "He just doesn't know anything modern. He's incredibly old-fashioned."

"Maybe—" Max started.

"I need to work with some real musicians," Amy went on, pacing. "Musicians my age who are into new music. I need some real rock and roll." She finished, doing a drum roll on the table with her hands.

"Maybe Sam can help," Palmer offered. Sam was Palmer's pen pal. "Sam and The Fantasy is the coolest band in Brighton. He's practically a national star—he was on television, remember? I know he could think of something."

Amy spun around to look at Palmer. "How could Sam help even if he wanted to? Boys aren't allowed on campus except under special circumstances. How could I hang out with Sam and his band?"

Palmer tossed her hair back and began drawing more hearts. Obviously, if Amy didn't appreciate her offer of Sam's help, then there was nothing more she could do.

"Maybe there are other girls here at Alma you could jam with," Shanon suggested. "I know Kate Majors plays an instrument and she—"

"Shanon, nothing against Kate as a person, but she's not cool," Amy answered. "I doubt she even knows who McHammer is."

"It was just an idea," said Shanon. None of her friends in the suite understood friendship with Kate Majors. They all thought Kate was strange.

"The only other girl who's into music is Brenda Smith. She's great, but she's too folksy and granola for me." Amy sighed loudly. "I'll just have to face facts. As long as I'm at

4

Alma Stephens, I have no freedom of choice. I can't sing the music I like with the people I want. I can't go to a concert or even a movie when I feel like it. I can't go to a record store."

"Or a department store," Palmer said, moving away from the window. "Or meet boys or go on a normal date like other normal fourteen-year-old girls."

"This place is a prison," Amy agreed.

"Worse than a prison. Here we don't even get any time off for good behavior," Palmer continued, beginning to enjoy this complaint fest.

"We're not in touch with the real world. There's no reality here," Amy declared.

"And no normal dating," Palmer repeated, pushing up the sleeves of her baby-blue cashmere sweater. "I haven't seen Sam for ages and ages. All I have are Sam's letters." Palmer draped herself across the loveseat. "I might as well be chained to my desk and fed bread and water."

"But at least Sam works at Figaro's," Shanon reminded Palmer. She hated to see her suitemates so unhappy. "We can always stop by for a visit when we get a town pass."

"The last time we did that Sam wasn't even there," Palmer complained. "Working as a messenger means he's always out delivering pizzas . . . to someone else."

"We could order pizza after pizza, hoping he'll be the messenger," Shanon said, giggling.

Max laughed also. "Can you imagine the room filled with pizza and Miss Pryn coming in?" The two roommates laughed louder at the thought of the headmistress surrounded by pizza!

"You two might think it's funny," Palmer huffed, "but

Valentine's Day is coming up in a few weeks. And if we were in a co-ed school, I could bump into Sam more frequently."

"So?" Max asked, still chuckling.

"Well, then he would have so many more opportunities to give me a valentine. He would have to—he would see me every day," Palmer explained. "As it is now, we just have the mail connecting the two of us and there's more of a chance for a letter or valentine to get lost."

"Oh, who cares about valentines," Amy said. "I wouldn't expect John to give me one. He's just my pen pal—not my boyfriend."

"That doesn't matter," said Maxie. "Valentine's Day is a chance for friends to say how much they care about each other."

"Especially *boy* friends," said Palmer. "What do you all think? If our pen pals don't send us valentines, should we send them valentines, anyway? I already have one picked out for Sam," she added.

"I don't think I could," Shanon began, turning slightly pink. "I mean, I would be so embarrassed if I sent one to Mars and he didn't send me one." Mars was Shanon's pen pal. They were very close friends, but Shanon wasn't sure if he felt anything more for her than that. "I once sent a boy in my third-grade class a valentine and he didn't give me one. He teased me about it for the rest of the year."

"You could always sent a valentine anonymously," Amy suggested. She kicked off her cowboy boots, revealing her PeeWee Herman socks. "That way, you won't be embarrassed if Sam doesn't send you one. And if he does send you one, you can let him know that the mysterious valentine is from you."

6

"I want a valentine from Sam and that's that!" Palmer insisted. "I want a big one with lots of hearts and I want him to sign it, 'With lots of love, Sam.' "

"Go for it, Palmer!" Shanon cheered.

"There might be a Valentine's Day Dance. If there is, I'll invite Sam. Of course, Amy will ask John and Shanon will invite Mars. Hmm." Palmer gazed at Max who hid behind her newspaper. "You can ask Paul Grant." Paul was the new boy who shared the suite with Mars, Rob, and John.

"I'll take care of myself," Max growled, scrunching down into the chair. She didn't want any of the other Foxes to know that she thought Paul Grant was kind of cute. If they knew they would never stop bugging her to become his pen pal. Boys just made her feel taller and bigger than she usually felt, and she especially didn't want to be awkward in front of someone like Paul. For now she was happy writing to nine-year-old Jose—a brilliant but troubled little boy she had befriended.

"But if Sam doesn't send me a card," Palmer continued, ignoring Max, "I don't know if I should still dance with him. I'll have to make sure I dance with all the other cute boys just to make him jealous." Palmer giggled. "There must be something I can do to make sure he sends me one—even if I have to spend the next three weeks hinting."

"I couldn't care less if John sends me one or not," Amy declared. "Besides, a card from John would probably be like one of his poems—weird."

"I thought you liked his poems!" Shanon sputtered, shocked. What was happening in the suite? Her suitemates were going crazy! Palmer was totally hung up on Sam, and Amy sounded as if she didn't care about John at all.

"I did. I do," Amy wailed. "But I just—maybe it's all the

7

snow—or the fact that it's almost February. I hate February! There's nothing to do or look forward to. It's only January twenty-seventh and already I feel like February's been here for five years." She began pacing again. "The holidays are all over and it's still winter and will be winter for the next fifty years. And everything is the same, same, same. I'm bored, bored, bored!" Amy chanted.

"Look at this!" Max blurted, jumping out of her seat. The three other girls looked over at her. " 'Local rock band looking for female lead singer and a male guitarist; all types are welcome,' " she read from the newspaper. She quickly scanned the ad and looked up at Amy, grinning. "The auditions are next Sunday, February first, and anyone is welcome to try out. Too bad you can't try out for that band, Amy."

The three girls turned to look at Amy. Amy put her hand on her chest. Her heart was beating rapidly. She knew this ad was a dream come true. "Why can't I? I could get a town pass and give it a shot."

"You know you could!" Max added.

"Do you really think so?" Amy said, beginning to back down. "I've never been to a professional audition before."

"The ad doesn't say anything about it being professional," Shanon said, taking the newspaper from Max's hands.

"It's probably just a bunch of kids," Palmer said flatly. "Sam and his group are professionals."

"Well, this group probably is too, Palmer," Max reasoned, "or they wouldn't have had the money to take out the ad."

Palmer took the newspaper from Shanon. "Would a pro-

8

fessional band put out an ad saying that absolutely anyone in the whole world could try out to be their lead singer?" Palmer asked, sitting down in the chair that Max had vacated. She examined her fingernail polish and continued, "I mean, if the band leader was really hot, wouldn't he or she know enough good singers already?"

"Not necessarily," Amy disagreed. She could feel the excitement growing in her stomach and she didn't want Palmer or anyone else to ruin it for her. Her annual February fog seemed to be lifting. "Maybe this band is looking for someone fresh. Maybe the band leader is cool enough to take a chance."

"On an unknown talent," Maxie exclaimed.

"Someone who nobody has ever heard of before!" Shanon piped in.

Palmer looked up from her nails and yawned. "Yeah, that does happen. Overnight success stories. But I always thought that kind of thing happened to people who are older than we are. Not fourteen-year-olds, you know."

"There are lots of bands with people our age in it. Remember Michael Jackson was only six when he started," Amy said.

"Stars get discovered as teenagers all the time," Maxie added.

"That's true," Palmer conceded. She was beginning to come around. "So, are you going to try out?"

All three girls turned to look at Amy, waiting for the answer.

"I—am I really good enough?"

"Remember how they loved you in England," Shanon gushed.

"What will I wear?"

"We'll all lend you clothes," Maxie offered. "You'll look great!"

"What will I sing?"

"The songs that Kringle won't let you sing," Palmer suggested.

"But—do I bring my own guitar or do I sing with the band? I mean, I don't know if I can."

"Amy, you won't know until you go," Shanon said quietly.

"Shanon's right! Go for it!" Max encouraged.

Now that her suitemates were all behind her, Amy could feel herself getting more scared and unsure. Maybe Kringle knew something she didn't. Maybe she couldn't sing rock; maybe she would only be good enough for lessons all her life. "What will Dan and Maggie say?" she asked. Dan and Maggie were their dorm advisors. "They may not think it's a good idea."

"They're cool," Max assured her. "They'll understand."

"Besides," Palmer maintained, "we don't have to tell them. We all have town passes coming to us. Next Sunday we'll bike in together, buy stuff at the drugstore, stop at Figaro's. . . ."

"Figaro's, huh? Just a casual stop, in case Sam might be there?" Shanon teased.

"Why not?" Palmer asked. "After that, we can all go to Amy's audition. Maybe Sam will even come. He's a rock musician himself. He'll probably know exactly what to do to help you get ready for the audition. He might even know the people holding the audition! Once they see that you know Sam, you're sure to get in," Palmer finished.

"I do want to go . . ." Amy began.

"Do it, Amy!"

"But, it's so different from singing around campus. This is a real audition with a real band. It's all so real!"

"And who was the one complaining that this place wasn't real?" Maxie reminded her, grinning. "This is exactly what you were dreaming of—a place to do your kind of music with your kind of people!"

"We'll be right there with you, Amy," Shanon assured her.

"Well, what do I have to lose?" Amy asked, grinning and crossing her fingers. She could feel the excitement bubbling up inside her.

Max ran into Amy's bedroom, returned with the guitar, and handed it to her. Amy bowed before she took the guitar. Then she put one foot on the chair and rested the guitar on her knee. Strumming loudly, she sang, "What does a girl have to lose? All she has to do is choose!"

"Yeah, yeah, yeah!" Maxie joined in.

"When you choose, you got nothin' to lose!" Amy sang.

"Absolutely nothin'!" the three girls echoed.

"So go for it and be a big hit!" Maxie yodeled.

"Go for it! Be a hit!" Shanon and Palmer repeated.

"I'll go for it and be a hit!" Amy sang, happy and excited. Somehow she was going to make it work!

CHAPTER TWO

Hey, Shanon

How would you feel about having a whole new pen pal? Well, not a whole new one. The old Mars with changes. I decided to do something about all the comments I get from my roommates about my size (or lack of size as they would say). So, I've started a new routine. I get up earlier and lift weights. I've even started jogging—all this exercise is killing me!!

Tell me what you think.

An Ex-Ninety-Pound Weakling,
Mars

Dear Mars

I'm not sure what to say. I think you're fine the way you are. . . .

Dear Mars,

If you want to build up your muscles, that sounds great.

Dear Mars,

I would hate getting up—just to exercise. I think exercising is so boring; I could never make myself do it every day. I think it's great that you're able to. But I also think you're just fine the way (or weigh—I'm starting to write like you) you are.

You know, the physical side of a person isn't everything. There is such a thing as brain power and you have lots of it. I don't know anyone else who comes up with as many ideas as you do.

I have to admit that I'm no jock. I always hated gym class, especially in my old school. I was always one of the last girls picked for teams. The only athletic thing I know how to do is bike.

Right now I'm exercising my brain. I'm doing something different in English class. I hope it turns out okay. We had to read Lord of the Flies, which I just hated. You know Mr. Griffith. He's a great teacher and his assignment was to write a diary as though we were one of the boys in the book. Normally, I would think it's a great project, but I didn't want to be anyone in that book. I felt so horrible reading the book. So I just couldn't do anything. And it's due this Friday.

I asked him for an extension today. Something I've never done—I was so nervous. I told him I wanted to try something different, and he didn't even ask me what it was. He just said, "Go ahead, I trust you." Isn't he great? And he gave me the extra time. I won't tell you about it until I hear what he thinks after I hand it in, but wish me luck.

Long live brain power!

Your pen pal,
Shanon

13

P.S. You know if it weren't for brains then we wouldn't be pen pals. It was Lisa who thought this idea up. So, obviously, brain power brought all of us together. Tell that to your roommates.

Shanon,

Thanks for your great letter. It made me feel better knowing that there's at least one member of the female population who appreciates intellectual muscles. I bet Ben Franklin couldn't lift one hundred pounds, but everyone listened to him.

Unfortunately, I can't stop now. Or at least I have to go on pretending to build up my "ceps," as in tri and bi. If not, my roommates will go back to their Neanderthal behavior.

Speaking of roommates, you know Paul Grant, the newest member of our suite. Well, I realized that although he won't admit it, he's really interested whenever one of us gets a letter from the Foxes. He always seems to be around whenever we open our letters.

But—and listen to (or read) this—he says he hates girls. I, for one, don't believe him for a moment. He always seems to be asking about Maxie, wondering if any of you mention her in your letters. And this is only from a glimpse at that great Halloween party at Alma. What does Max think of Paul?

Write back soon. I have to go back and run around the track a few million times. It's so hard being the amazing
Mighty Mars

P.S. Good luck with your paper. I'm sure it will be great and I can't wait to hear what you decided to do.

14

Dear Palmer,

Big news in the O'Leary family. My older sister, Deirdre, is off to Europe in just a couple of days. She's traveling for a month. We're all going to go to the airport with her.

It's real exciting—she's the first one in our family to go abroad, but she won't be the last. I definitely want to travel more than anything. Brighton High has a summer work/study program in Europe that I'm going to apply to. Can you imagine it if I get accepted? It would be so fantastic. I bet I can travel and play music, meeting musicians all over the world.

Life is dreary here in Brighton. All I have to brighten up my thoughts are dreams.

Your lonely pen pal,
Sam

Dear Sam,

I can't even remember the first time I flew in an airplane or went to Europe. I don't mean this in a bad way. It must be nice to be so excited about flying and traveling. To think I was too young to even know what I was doing.

I'll miss you if you go to Europe. Then we'll definitely be long-distance pen pals. It will take forever for us to get mail from each other.

I wish Alma would sponsor a summer abroad program. Then maybe we could be in the same place in Europe and go to school together. Wouldn't that be cool? We wouldn't have to wait for dances or town passes to see each other. Maybe I'll write to the Wanda column about this.

How is The Fantasy doing? I just love your music. You and your band are just the coolest sound in Brighton. Probably in the United States. You know, if you all traveled together as a band in Europe, I bet you would be the best there, also.

Amy is going to an audition this Sunday. She's trying out to be a singer in a rock band in Brighton; they advertised in the newspaper for singers and musicians. Did you see it?

Is that how you got your band together? By advertising? Or did you know everyone first?

Anyway, the audition is this Sunday at one o'clock. All the Foxes are going with her for moral support, but first we're going to stop at Figaro's. Maybe we'll get to see each other.

Hope to see you Sunday,
Palmer

P.S. I was having this philosophical discussion with the other Foxes about Valentine's Day and valentines. You know, how it all started—the practice of giving valentines to people you care about. How do you think it started and what do you think about giving valentines? We're collecting opinions.

Dear Maxie,

Hi, how are you? I have big news for you. I have a girl freind. There is this girl in my class who I like a lot. I think she likes me, but I'm not sure.

Since your a girl too I was wondering what shuld I do to get this girl to like me back? What wuld make you like a boy? She's very pretty. Do you have any ideas? Her name is Hilary.

Jose

16

Dear Jose,

What do you mean you have a girlfriend? Who is she? Is she nice? Is she smart? Tell me more.

If I were you, I would forget about girls right now. You're only nine years old. I'm fourteen, five years older than you, and I'm not anyone's girlfriend and probably won't be for years!

You have a lot of other things to think about. Such as basketball and your spelling. Thinking about girls will only take time away from all these important things.

Write back soon,
Maxie

Dear Amy,

Isn't February a wonderful month? It's my favorite and it's almost here. It's one of those months that just is—with nothing special happening. Everyone can just go and do whatever they want without being interrupted. And I love the snow and cold. If I were a bear I would love February because I could just roll over and go back to sleep. Unfortunately, at Ardsley, they don't believe in hibernation and I have to study.

An Ode to February
Gray, snowy, and cold
Leaves buried by forgotten memories.
Ancient ghosts hover in the sky;
Death is around the corner.

Let me know how you're doing. I haven't heard from you in a while. Well, it's back to the books for me.

John

17

Dear Shanon,

Help! Help! Help! The snow and cold never stop here in Pennsylvania. What's the action at Alma?

Nothing is going on here really. Life is pretty boring. I go to school, study, go to school. My mom works and comes home. I need some excitement. Or maybe it's good that everything is quiet here for a change.

A new girl just came into my class last week. It's nice in a way for me because now I don't feel like the new kid anymore. Also, I can be helpful to someone else since I know what it feels like not to know anyone or anything.

I just heard from Rob. He says Mars is on this new exercise thing. Leave it to Mars to try anything once.

Write me. Write me. Write me. Say hi to the rest of the Foxes for me and tell them to write.

Love,
Lisa

CHAPTER THREE

" 'It isn't easy being me. But when the birds are singing and the sun is shining, there ain't no reason to be whining!' " Max sang at the top of her voice as the four Foxes bicycled down the long drive of Alma Stephens toward town on Sunday.

"What in the world was *that*?" Amy teased as she pedaled rapidly to catch up with her suitemate.

"You're not the only song writer around here," Max retorted. "And you have to admit that this is a beautiful day. Sunny, not a cloud in the sky."

"And cold," Palmer added, although she was dressed in a stylish dark-blue down jacket that looked great with her blond hair and blue eyes.

"Did you tell Maggie and Dan why we were going to town today?" Shanon asked, pedaling to keep up with her friends.

"No," Amy answered slowly. "I know they're cool and all that, but the fewer people who know, the fewer I have to tell that I flopped."

"You'll do great, Amy! Get the word *flop* out of your

mind," Shanon advised her as the four girls turned onto the road and off the school grounds.

"With your looks, energy, and voice, the band leader would have to be an idiot not to take you on," Maxie pronounced.

"Besides, you're a Fox and the Foxes are the best at whatever they do!" Palmer exclaimed.

Amy grinned as she shifted gears. "Well, with the fan club I have, they'll have to give me the gig."

The four girls bicycled in silence as they concentrated on breathing and pedaling in the cold air. Soon, they were in the center of town and had to watch for traffic.

"I'm thirsty," Palmer mentioned at a stoplight. "How about stopping for a soda before we get to the audition. Your throat must be dry, Amy."

"Isn't Figaro's just down the block?" Maxie asked, winking at Shanon.

"Why yes, it is," Palmer answered, looking around innocently. Her three friends burst out laughing. First she looked offended and then Palmer joined them. "Well, why not stop for a moment. Maybe Sam is there and we can get something to drink."

"Sounds fine to me," Amy said, "but only for a few minutes."

After the four girls parked their bikes outside of Figaro's, Amy and Palmer went in, taking Shanon's and Max's drink order. After a few moments, Amy came out with three drinks.

"Where's Palmer?" Shanon asked, sipping her root beer through a straw. She had pulled off her knitted hat, and her brown hair glinted in the sunlight.

"Sam wasn't there so she's finding out when he'll be back," Amy answered, looking at her watch.

"How do you feel, Amy?" Maxie asked in between slurps.

"Fine . . . actually, nervous beyond belief. But glad . . . and scared. Everything, I think, except calm."

"Stage fright is good, my father says. Gives you energy."

"He's on a delivery, but he'll be back soon," Palmer said, coming out of the shop. "Let's wait."

Amy shook her head, tossing her soda can into the recycling bin. "No, I have to get to this audition as soon as possible. You can see Sam anytime and today is the only day for the audition, and it's first come, first audition, starting at one o'clock and it's one-fifteen now."

"But Sam can probably help you at the audition," Palmer asserted. "He can put in a good word for you."

"I don't need Sam. I need to get to that audition now. You agreed to stop for only a few minutes. We've been here for ten minutes. Let's go," Amy said, swinging her leg over her bike.

"I agree with Amy, Palmer," Maxie said. "Today is the audition—that's the whole reason we're here."

"Come on, Palmer. You can send Sam a note that you stopped by," Shanon suggested.

Shanon and Max threw their sodas away and got on their bikes. Palmer just stood by herself, her unopened soda in her hand, uncertain.

"Let's go," Amy demanded, putting her foot on the pedal.

"Wait!" Palmer said as she put her soda in her knapsack and got on her bike. "I'm coming with you guys. Your

21

audition is more important, I guess . . . this time. . . ."

"Amy, will you have time tonight to help me with my math?" Palmer asked as they bicycled together ahead of Max and Shanon.

"Sure, I guess," Amy answered, distracted. She was imagining herself at Madison Square Garden, singing before thousands of screaming fans.

"You promised."

"I know. I said I will and I will. But now I want to concentrate on the audition. Okay?"

"Okay," Palmer finally agreed. "But I'll remind you tonight."

"I wish they would bike faster," Amy murmured, glancing behind her.

"Shanon, how's your paper going?" Max asked. She and Shanon were a half a block behind Palmer and Amy.

Shanon made a face. "Well, I have to get it in by Wednesday. I'm a little nervous because I want Mr. Griffith to really like it, but it's different from anything else I ever tried," Shanon explained. "It's also a lot longer than the paper was originally supposed to be. I'm on page fifteen and I'm not even halfway finished with it."

"I'm sure it will be great," Max said encouragingly.

"Let's not talk about it any more today, all right? I want to forget it for now." Maxie nodded her agreement. "See that house, Maxie," Shanon exclaimed, pointing to a big, red-brick house. "That's where the vice-principal of the junior high lives. Every Halloween the kids toilet-paper his house. Doreen told me that Mr. Sperling would come in on November first looking utterly exhausted, as though he

22

had stayed up all night, but he never caught any of the kids in all these years."

"Can you imagine if we tried to paper Miss Pryn," Maxie said.

"She would take away all our privileges."

"And make us have tea every day," Max groaned, hating the tea ritual with Miss Pryn, for she was always worried she would break something.

"Max, we're getting near the house where the audition is being held," Shanon said. "Amy, what's the address?"

"It's on Clinton Place—487 Clinton Place," Amy called back.

"Make the next left." The four girls followed Shanon's directions and soon they stopped in front of the house. They all stared at the three-story white house with the wraparound porch. The porch looked deserted except for an old swing, creaking in the slight breeze.

"Maybe it was a joke ad, you know?" Amy whispered, her voice quavering. The house looked empty; the shades were drawn, and the paint was chipping off. "Do you know who lives here, Shanon?"

"No," Shanon answered, shaking her head. "I know Mrs. Cytron three houses down and the Finellis live across the street. But I don't know who lives here."

Amy clapped her hand to her mouth. "Maybe we got the address wrong." The girls stared at one another and then silently at the house again.

"I don't even hear any music," Amy mumbled.

"Well, all you can do is knock on the door and find out," Shanon suggested.

"Go ahead, Amy," Maxie encouraged.

23

"Right. I'm here to audition and nothing's going to stop me now," Amy declared suddenly.

She pedaled down the front path to the bottom steps of the house and parked her bike. Looking back, she gave a thumbs-up to her friends. Then Amy climbed the porch steps, walked up to the front door, and knocked loudly.

Suddenly the door opened and a blast of rock and roll poured out the door. This was definitely the place!

CHAPTER FOUR

—————◆—————

Shanon, Palmer, and Max heard the blast of music before they saw the young boy who answered the door. They grinned at one another; this house was rocking. They locked up theirs and Amy's bikes and joined her at the front door.

She turned around with a big smile on her face. The boy had already disappeared into the house.

"This is it," Amy shouted, grabbing their hands. "That kid said that Emmett—he's the leader of the band—is downstairs listening to people right now. I have to put my name on a sign-up sheet."

"Let's go!"

The four girls entered the old house, Max shutting the door behind them. Everywhere she looked she saw kids—sprawled on the floor, sitting on chairs, couches, window seats, leaning against walls, or just standing.

"This is too much," Maxie whispered to Shanon, who just nodded.

"I'm going to find the list," Amy told them.

"We'll meet you in that space," Maxie said, pointing to

a small, clear area on the floor. Leading the way, she pushed through the crowd and claimed the space quickly with Palmer and Shanon trailing behind her.

"You obviously come from New York," Shanon commented, admiringly.

"I didn't realize that there would be this many people," Palmer said, sitting on her jacket so she wouldn't get her jeans dirty.

"I wonder why the guys all have guitars and the girls don't," Shanon said, still staring at everything around her.

"I think it's because the girls are trying out for lead singer and the guys for musician. It did say in the ad that they wanted a *female* singer," Max answered. "I wonder if Emmett's the kind of guy who thinks only boys can play the instruments and girls are only able to sing."

"Don't mention that to Amy," Shanon warned. "We want her to audition, not get upset because the lead guy may be unfair."

"I found the list and my name is at the bottom," Amy announced, sitting next to Palmer. "This is so exciting, but I don't see anyone I recognize. No one from Ardsley or Alma."

"Probably just the Brighton High crowd. Maybe that means that Sam will show up. I hope so. I did tell him all about Amy's audition in my letter."

"You what?" Amy exclaimed. "Palmer, I wanted this to be private. Do you have to tell Sam O'Leary everything— even stuff that is my business? It's bad enough that you made us stop at Figaro's before we came here. If we hadn't, I wouldn't be so far down on the list. Now, we might have to leave before they even get to me."

"Sam's a good person to tell about your audition,"

Palmer insisted knowingly. "He's into rock and roll."

"So are a lot of people, but that doesn't mean anything. Just because you like Sam doesn't mean he's the only one in town with musical talent. Just look at the crowd in this place," Amy continued, waving her arm to demonstrate and practically hitting the girl next to her. "Oops, sorry."

"It's okay. It is kind of squishy in here. I don't think they could fit anyone else in. I'm Julie," the wide-eyed girl said, laughing.

"I'm Amy. This place is amazing. What's the name of the group?" Amy asked.

"Emmett and the Heartbreak. I hear they're great."

"Have you ever heard them before?" Palmer questioned. The girl shook her head no. "Have you ever heard of Sam O'Leary?"

"Oh, yeah, Sam and The Fantasy, right?" Julie asked. "They were on television."

"I know," Palmer answered with a satisfied smile on her face. Amy rolled her eyes and began talking with another girl next to her.

"*No! No! No!* Get lost! I don't want to hear any more!" Abruptly the music from downstairs stopped.

"Who's that?" Shanon asked.

"Sounds like it's coming from the basement," Amy answered, grabbing Shanon's arm.

"Can't anybody sing in this lousy town!" the boy's angry voice continued.

Instantly the room got quieter. To everyone's surprise, an older, gray-haired woman came in from another room. Shanon almost giggled with nervousness, for the woman was wearing an old-fashioned apron with ruffles and her hair was up in a bun; she definitely didn't belong at a rock and roll audition. The woman carefully picked her way through the crowd and stood at the head of the basement steps.

"Everything okay, Emmett?" she called down, drying her hands on her apron.

"Yeah, Aunt Claire!" the boy called back up.

"Well, let me know if you need anything."

"Okay." With that answer, she turned around, walked through the crowd, and disappeared through the kitchen door.

"Who's that?" Amy gasped.

"I think she's his aunt," Julie replied. "Somebody told me she's incredible. She lets Emmett do anything he wants. He's turned her entire basement into a music studio."

"Wow!" Amy exclaimed, taking a big breath. "A whole music studio. . . . Awesome!"

"I wonder how long this is going to take," Palmer started to complain. She stopped when she heard footsteps clomping up the basement stairs. A tall, skinny, dark-haired boy appeared in the front hallway, wearing sunglasses even though it was quite dark in the house.

"That's Emmett," another girl next to them whispered.

"He's old," Palmer gasped.

"He must be seventeen or older," Amy exclaimed admiringly. "He's totally cool-looking."

Not looking at anyone, Emmett strutted into the living room. He even ignored the boy who had just auditioned and was now trying to sneak unnoticed out the front door. Palmer watched as most of the kids in the room greeted Emmett and he ignored them. She knew there would be no way she would ever say hi to someone who didn't pay attention to her first.

The kid who answered the door rushed up to Emmett with the list in his hand. "Here's the sheet, Emmett. The next person is—"

"What do I need this for?" Emmett ripped the list as he snatched it out of the boy's hand. He looked around the room over the top of his glasses and stopped as he focused on the Foxes. Palmer felt Amy grab her hand. "You!" he demanded pointing at Amy. "What's your name?"

"Amy—Amy Ho," she answered clearly despite her nervousness.

"Come on down and let's see what you can do," he instructed. "I like your looks." Without waiting for an answer, he turned around and went back downstairs.

"Go on, you heard Emmett," the younger kid said.

"Wish me luck," Amy whispered to her suitemates, and she scrambled up off the floor and followed Emmett down the stairs.

"Gosh, he's been picking people at random all day," Julie complained, taking a novel out of her knapsack. "What's the point of having a list? I'm tenth on the list and he stopped going in order after the fifth one."

"Let's go listen to Amy sing," Shanon suggested.

"Good idea. Good luck, Julie," Maxie offered. Walking to the top of the basement steps, they could hear the music starting up.

"This band is so loud I can't even hear Amy's voice," Shanon said.

"I don't like this sound. It's not mellow like The Fantasy," Palmer complained.

"Shhh," Maxie demanded.

The music stopped, and Shanon heard voices, but she couldn't make out the words. Suddenly there was silence

29

and then the sound of one guitar playing. Shanon heard a familiar voice accompanying the guitar. It was Amy singing—her audition had begun!

CHAPTER FIVE

"So tell us again what happened once you went downstairs," Shanon insisted. The Foxes were sitting together in the dining hall Monday morning eating breakfast.

Amy had barely touched her food she was so excited; she felt as if she were starring in her own movie.

"Well, I followed him down the stairs and there were two other guys there," Amy began, her eyes shining. She grinned at Shanon and Max who were sitting forward in their seats, leaning closer to her. "Emmett played lead guitar of course—"

"I thought he was kind of cute," Max said. "He reminds me of guys from New York."

"What did he look like up close and personal?" Shanon asked.

"I don't know. I didn't really notice, although he did have these incredible green eyes. Not as light as a cat's eyes, but more like the dark green of a forest. And the longest black eyelashes—why do the guys always have the great eyelashes?"

"And you say you didn't notice?" Maxie teased.

"Well, I couldn't help but notice. They were so unusual."

"I think you like him," Shanon said with a laugh.

"I do not. It's totally professional. He just happens to be cute in addition to being talented," Amy protested. "Anyway, there was a drummer and a guy on the keyboards. They're looking for someone to play bass guitar. Then, once we got down there, Emmett became all business. He told them to take it from the top and handed me song lyrics. First he asked me to sing and then he sang it for me, playing the guitar so I could hear how the song went. He was incredible. I don't know which I liked more—his singing or his playing. It was an old song, but he sang it in a way I had never heard before. Then he asked me to sing it again and he was thrilled by the fact that I could pick it up so quickly."

"We always knew you were a genius," Shanon declared, slurping her orange juice.

"So I sang all three songs. I had the best time singing; the guys in the band smiled at me the whole time and nodded, just like they do in real bands. It wasn't like my lessons with Kringle. I had fun and just sang out exactly how I felt. Then Emmett asked me if I had any original songs I could sing.

"So I sang 'Cabin Fever' and he loved it. He asked me to do it twice."

"Amy, I have to leave for class soon," Palmer said, gathering her books. "We are meeting today so you can help me study for tomorrow's math quiz since you couldn't help me last night, right?"

"Sure, sure," Amy answered quickly. "This is the good part."

"But, Amy—"

"What happened next?" Shanon asked.

"Shanon, we heard this all last night. She sang standing on top of a table," Palmer said, annoyed.

"I want to hear it again!" Shanon insisted, shushing Palmer.

"But my quiz—"

"Then he told me to stand on top of the table while I sang." Amy told them.

"That is so cool!" Maxie added.

"He told me to just let go. To see what came to me! That I had complete freedom to do or try anything I wanted to do."

"Sounds great, Amy. Real different from Kringle," Max said, laughing.

"I think it sounds stupid," Palmer stated flatly, pushing her chair back. The three girls stared at her. "Suppose what you want to do sounds real bad? Are you supposed to do that just because you feel like it? In Sam's band, all the numbers are planned. They know just—"

"Here we go with Sam again!" Amy interrupted. "Does Sam have to be in every conversation? Not everyone is interested in your pen pal!"

"You used to be," Palmer replied quickly. "You used to show us your letters from John, too. I know you got one from John on Saturday and you still haven't told us what he said."

"Yikes, I forgot all about it. I haven't even opened it yet," Amy gasped, pulling the letter out from her notebook.

"How could you not open it right away, Amy? I always open mine from Mars immediately, no matter what."

"Open it now," Maxie directed.

33

Dear Amy,

Hi, I'm writing again even though I didn't hear from you after my last letter. I figured maybe you're just too busy with school so I thought you might need a break from the ol' grind. Did you like my February poem? Here's another in a completely different style.

> *At night the moon glows brightly,*
> *My dreams are filled with colors*
> *Yet there is something I am missing.*
> *Hours pass and I feel empty.*
> *Oh, only if I could find the key.*

Tell me what you think, but don't be too hard on me. I'm trying to broaden my horizons, you know.

Poetically yours,
John

"Gosh, Amy, I really like that poem," Palmer exclaimed, leaning over her roommate. "It's the first one that means something to me."

"Look, it spells Amy Ho," Shanon pointed out.

"What do you think he's trying to say?" Maxie teased.

"I think he really likes you," Palmer said.

"Oh, it's just John being John. It's not one of his best," Amy said airily, stuffing the letter into her bag.

"Well, you'd better tell him you like it anyway," Palmer advised. "I'm on the social committee and if I have anything to do about it, the Valentine's Day Dance is a definite."

"Can we invite Ardsley boys?" Shanon asked immediately.

"Why have it if we can't?" Palmer countered.

"When?"

"February fourteenth, of course. I have to meet with the committee, but I'm sure we can invite whomever we want."

"I'm definitely inviting Mars. What about you, Max?"

Twisting her straw in her hands, Max kept her eyes down. "Do I have to invite someone?"

"No, of course not," Shanon said soothingly. "But it would be nice."

"What about Paul Grant?" Palmer suggested.

"I already said no." Max's voice shook a little. "I don't even know him. Anyway, if I don't have to invite anybody to the dance, then I'm not going to."

"But the rest of us are going to have dates. Shanon will be with Mars; I'll be with Sam; Amy will—"

"I may not have a date," Amy announced.

"What are you talking about?" Shanon asked, alarmed. "We always invite our pen pals to anything that goes on."

"I might not even go to the dance. I may not have the time," Amy explained, lifting up her chin and sitting straighter in her chair. "If I get the job with the band, I may have rehearsals. Or even a gig."

"Come on, Amy. If you do get the job, you can't rehearse at night. You wouldn't be allowed." Amy didn't respond so Palmer continued. "Besides, if you are going to get hired, how come Emmett didn't tell you at the auditions?"

"He needs to see me again!" Amy declared. "It isn't easy picking out the lead singer; it's a big decision."

35

"Well, I hope you don't get it," Palmer stated.

"What!" Max and Shanon shouted at the same time.

"Palmer, how could you? You know Amy wants this more than anything!" Shanon sputtered.

"You're not being funny," Maxie said.

"I'm not trying to be funny." Palmer tossed her hair back elegantly with her manicured right hand. "I'm saying this for Amy's own good. I think that Emmett guy is a creep! His music doesn't sound good, for one thing. He was yelling at everyone. Being mean, even to his aunt. And his hair was filthy!" Palmer finished.

"That's crazy! Hair doesn't mean anything!" Shanon answered.

"Come to New York and you'll see that the most talented people have dirty hair. They have more important things to think about—like their art!" Max explained.

"Look at Einstein! Or at Beethoven! Do you think they cared how their hair looked!" Amy asked in disbelief. "Genius has nothing to do with hair, clean or dirty!" Amy stood up and gathered her books. "I have to get to class. See you later," Amy said as she left the table.

"Palmer, don't you think you were kind of mean to Amy," Shanon suggested.

"Well, his hair *was* dirty," Palmer muttered to herself, following Max and Shanon out of the dining hall.

CHAPTER SIX

Sitting in Mr. Griffith's class, Shanon worried. She worried about her paper, which she had to hand in this Wednesday, and she worried about Palmer and Amy. She couldn't believe that Palmer didn't want Amy to get the job. She knew Palmer could be difficult and selfish, but never this selfish. She looked at Maxie who was sitting diagonally across from her and then up at Mr. Griffith. He was discussing *Lord of the Flies* as usual.

I really don't have to listen since I'm not doing the paper he assigned, Shanon thought. She started to write in her notebook:

Max,
    What do you think of Palmer? I couldn't believe some of the stuff she said.

Shanon

Ripping the paper as quietly as possible, Shanon folded the note and passed it over to Max. She watched Max unfold it, read it, and then write her own note.

Shanon,

It's typical Palmer, but I would be really annoyed at her if I were Amy. It's bad enough acting like someone's really weird if they don't want to ask someone to a dance, but then to tell Amy that she hopes she doesn't get the job was too much.

Max

Max,

Palmer doesn't think you're weird because you don't want to go to the dance. You know she just says things without thinking. I just hope Amy remembers that.

Shanon

"Shanon." It was Mr. Griffith standing above her as she finished passing the note to Max.

"Y-yes, Mr. Griffith," Shanon answered, her face bright red.

"Please see me after class," he began.

"After class?" Shanon asked, seeing Max look at her sympathetically.

"Yes, so we can discuss your paper. Is something wrong?" Mr. Griffith asked.

"No," Shanon said, relief filling her voice. "I'm fine." As Mr. Griffith turned away, Shanon let out a big gasp of air and slumped in her seat. Max gave her a small thumbs-up.

For Shanon, the period went slower than ever as she wondered what Mr. Griffith wanted to say to her. At the end of class, she stood in front of Mr. Griffith's desk, shifting her weight from side to side.

Mr. Griffith looked up at her and smiled. "Calm down,

Shanon. I just want to know how you're doing on your paper."

"I guess okay," she answered uncertainly.

"It is due this Wednesday, you know. Will you have it finished in two days?"

"I—I . . ." Shanon pushed her hair off her face and took a deep breath to calm down. "Actually, Mr. Griffith, I don't think it will be done. It's taking me a lot longer than I thought. I'm already on page twenty and I can't even see the end."

"Well," he said, chuckling slightly, "please stop before you get to one hundred. I do have to have time to read it. I won't ask exactly what you're doing. I'm just pleased you're so involved in it. I look forward to reading it. What if I give you until next Wednesday? Will that be enough time?"

"Oh, yes, thanks, Mr. Griffith." Shanon practically beamed at him.

"I'll see you tomorrow, then," Mr. Griffith said.

"Right, thanks again." Shanon turned to leave.

"Oh, by the way, Shanon," Mr. Griffith said, not looking up from the papers he had begun to grade.

"Yes?"

"Don't be so obvious about passing notes. If you do it right out as though you hadn't a care in the world, I probably would never notice it. That method always worked for me."

"Yes, Mr. Griffith," Shanon answered, grinning as she left the room.

Palmer walked into history class and noticed that Amy

was already in her seat, talking to Brenda Smith. Normally, Amy would wave or even stop talking to greet her roomie, but she didn't today. *It's as if I don't even exist,* Palmer thought to herself. *Well, just because I'm right about Emmett, she's annoyed.* Palmer sat down right next to Amy, but she could have been sitting in Alaska for all the attention Amy paid her.

Halfway through history, Palmer ripped out a small piece of paper and thought for a moment.

Amy,

Sorry about this morning. You know I'm not really awake that early.

I'm free between seven and eight-thirty tonight, so you can help me with my math.

Your roomie,
Palmer

Palmer slipped the note onto Amy's desk. Amy read the note, wrote on the back of it, and then tossed it back on Palmer's desk when the teacher wasn't looking.

P—

I don't want to hear anything bad about Emmett again. You are entitled to your own feelings. They're yours, but don't tell me. I'm rehearsing my singing tonight.

A

Palmer read the note and ripped it into small pieces. *Fine,* she thought, *if that's how she feels. I don't need her help anyway. I have Sam and I don't need anyone else.*

40

Palmer folded her arms and made herself a promise. She would prove to Amy that she was right about Emmett, no matter what it took. That creep!

CHAPTER SEVEN

Shanon looked up from her English paper. Amy sat across from her at the table, chewing on her pencil as she worked on her math problems. Max sat in the loveseat, reading her history book and a novel at the same time. Palmer was curled up in the chair, memorizing French verbs, mouthing them silently.

It all looked normal—the Foxes were all together, studying. But Shanon knew it wasn't quite normal. Palmer was acting more sure of herself than ever and Amy was ignoring her. Life in 3-D wasn't fun right now and fun was one of the things the Foxes did best together.

Maybe something will happen soon that will bring everything back to the way it was, Shanon hoped silently.

"Can I come in?" It was Georgette Durand, opening the door and walking in without waiting for an answer. Shanon groaned to herself; Georgette, Palmer's stepsister, always put Palmer in a bad mood. "Hi, everyone! I have the most exciting news," Georgette announced. She was so much like Palmer, from her bright blue eyes to her blond

42

hair to her stylish and feminine clothes to her self-centeredness. The only difference Shanon saw between them besides the fact that Georgette was a year younger was that Georgette was a brilliant student and Palmer had to really work to get good grades.

"Hi, Georgette," Shanon replied when she saw that Palmer barely looked up from her book.

"You'll never guess, Palmer!" Georgette continued, walking over to her sister and pulling the French book away from her.

"What is it?" Palmer finally asked in an annoyed voice.

"I have it on the utmost authority that there will be a Valentine's Day Dance! Isn't that great!" Georgette practically squeaked.

"How do you know that?" Palmer demanded, finally giving Georgette all her attention.

"Well, Reid Olivier told me. Her class decided to take it over from the social committee. Her class is sponsoring it. Anyway, Reid is in charge."

"What?" Palmer gasped. "I thought the social committee was doing this dance! I'm on the social committee! How come I didn't know this?"

"Well, the way Reid explained it to me was that she and some of her classmates went to Miss Pryn and Miss Pryn gave them special permission."

"Just think of all the work you don't have to do, Palmer," Max reminded her, grinning at Shanon and Amy.

"That's true," Palmer conceded, calming down a little. "If we were giving it, I would have to work during the dance. This way I can just enjoy the dance."

"How did you get all this information?" Max asked Georgette.

The younger girl just smiled. "I have friends in all the right places. Reid tells me everything."

"I wouldn't trust Reid so quickly," Palmer warned Georgette, glad to give her sister advice and tell her what to do. "Why would a fifth-former like Reid be friends with a third-former like you?"

"Just because—" Max started.

"Well, I am mature for my age," Georgette interrupted, happy to have her sister's attention. "Anyway, I thought you could advise me on how to get a date for the dance."

"Ask some boy," Palmer answered and then opened up her French book and began reading again.

"But I don't know anyone around here," Georgette whined.

"Don't look at me," Max responded. "I'm not going with a date."

"I probably won't either. Sorry," Amy finally said when it seemed evident that Palmer wouldn't say anything.

"I will—probably," Shanon admitted quickly, "but I wouldn't know how to help you get one. There will be lots of boys from Ardsley there to dance with. You don't have to go with someone in order to dance or have a good time. You can meet someone there."

Georgette stuck out her lower lip and stared at Palmer's bent head. "I had hoped that a certain person would be more concerned about another certain person's social welfare, but obviously she is not," she said haughtily. "That is surprising since I am always on the lookout for ways to help this certain person. Since I am such 'good' friends with Reid, I suggested a certain band play that night—a certain Sam and The Fantasy."

44

"You what?" Palmer exploded, throwing her French book down. "How could you?"

"I thought you would like that," Georgette squeaked nervously.

"If anyone has the right to ask Sam to play at an Alma Stephens dance, I do. Besides, if Sam's band is the entertainment, then how could he possibly be my date? Did you ever think of that, Ms. Know-It-All?" Palmer exclaimed, two bright pink spots appearing on her cheeks.

"N-no," Georgette said, looking as if she were about to cry. "I didn't think of that. I just thought you would be so happy to be able to give Sam a job. I'm sorry. Really. Anyway, no one has actually asked him yet, so it's not too late."

"That's good," Palmer grumbled, picking up her book.

"I know a band you can recommend," Amy piped up suddenly. "Emmett and the Heartbreak. They're absolutely fresh."

"I never heard of them." Georgette turned toward Amy.

"They're the best," Amy said with a quick glance at Palmer. "They do real rock and roll music. Great music with a heavy beat. Emmett—he's the lead—is older and really cool. He looks like a real rock and roll star."

"How can you tell? Real rock stars don't wash their hair?" Palmer muttered.

"They would be great at the dance," Amy concluded.

"Sounds good," Georgette agreed. "I'll tell Reid about them. Emmett and the Heartbreak—I love the name." Georgette looked around and saw that Palmer still looked really angry. Gulping slightly, she walked toward the door. "Well, I guess I'd better go. If anyone does think of a way for me to get a date, I'll be in my room." Seeing that Palmer still didn't respond, she added, "Maybe I'll just ask Reid since *she's* so nice to me. And thanks, Amy, for the suggestion. I'll make sure that Reid really considers the Heartbreak."

The moment the door closed, Palmer sprang up from her chair and burst out, "Why does she always have to act as if she knows it all! She makes me so mad! Sticking her nose in places where it doesn't belong. She doesn't even know enough to realize that Reid's just using her. She makes me so mad. And why didn't you two"—she pointed to Amy and Shanon—"back me up on Reid—you know how underhanded she is."

"But, Palmer—" Shanon tried to interrupt.

"And another thing, how could you recommend Emmett for the dance when Sam might be available?"

"Palmer!" Amy exclaimed, looking at her two other suitemates in exasperation. "Since you don't want Sam to do it, why not let Emmett have a chance?"

"I could understand if you're doing this because you like Emmett like I like Sam. But then I can't imagine anyone having a crush on someone like Emmett." Palmer wrinkled up her nose.

"I don't have time right now to explain that I do not have a crush on Emmett. It's all business between us," Amy said, turning slightly pink. She closed her notebook, went into her room, and returned with her jacket. "I have more important things to do."

"Where are you going, Amy?" Maxie asked, looking at her watch. "It's six-thirty."

"I'm going to practice my singing. I have another audition with Emmett on Thursday, and I want to be ready. He wanted to see me again, remember? Well, Thursday's the day!"

"Amy, that's great!" Maxie cheered, giving her suitemate a hug.

"Yeah, that's great! When on Thursday? Don't you have a lesson with Kringle?" Shanon worried, for it got dark so early in New Hampshire.

"Four o'clock," Amy announced. "Well, I have to go."

"You *are* going to tell Maggie and Dan, aren't you?" Shanon pushed.

"No, not really," Amy admitted slowly, not looking at her friends. "I was just going to bike into town and be back by six at the latest."

"I think you should tell them," Shanon insisted.

"I just don't want to use up another town pass. I might need them later, especially if I join the band."

"I think Shanon's right, Amy. Don't sneak out," Maxie advised.

Amy looked at her two suitemates and then smiled. "Okay. How about if I just tell them I need some stuff from the pharmacy. That way they know I'm in town, but I don't have to use up a pass or tell them where I'm really going."

"You drive a hard bargain, Amy Ho, but I guess that will do. What do you think, Shanon?"

Shanon tried to look stern, but she couldn't keep it up. "Sounds good to me. I'll walk out with you, Amy. I need to work on my paper at the library. I'm not getting anywhere closer to the end."

"Wait for me," Max said. "I'm never going to finish reading history with this novel in the same room. I might as well join you, Shanon, for the grind. Then we can stop and get some hot chocolate as a treat." Shanon and Maxie went into their room to get their coats and books together, leaving Amy and Palmer alone in the sitting room. Amy started whistling an old Beatles tune, drumming on the tabletop while Palmer went back to her French book. Each girl avoided the other's eyes.

Palmer peered over her French book and noticed that Amy was just staring into space, her eyes dreamy. She smiled smugly to herself and was sure that Amy was thinking of Emmett, although she couldn't ever dream of wanting to kiss someone like him.

"Ready!" Maxie announced, walking back into the room.

"See you later, Palmer!" Shanon called back as the three girls left the suite.

Palmer threw her French book down and rushed to the window. Standing alone, she watched Shanon, Amy, and Max clown around as they walked together.

Not only don't they understand my side of anything, Palmer thought, *but Amy is acting so differently. Ever since she met Emmett, she hasn't done anything she normally does. She doesn't help me study anymore and I bet I failed that math test because of her. And she's going off to town on Thursday without permission. She never does that.*

Palmer watched her suitemates until she couldn't see them anymore. She wandered into her room and flopped on her bed. Lying on her stomach, she pulled Sebastian, her favorite teddy bear, closer to her.

"How dare she say Emmett is *real* rock and roll and suggest that Sam isn't!" she said out loud and then laughed. "If you keep talking aloud to yourself or to Sebastian,

Palmer Durand, everyone's going to think you're nuts!"

Thinking of Emmett, Palmer shivered. She just didn't like him. And she knew she was right about him and his band. They were all creepy. She just needed to prove it and show Amy, Shanon, and Max that she was right. *Who else would know him or know about him,* Palmer thought. *Sam! They both live in Brighton and are both musicians.*

"Sam will know!" Palmer declared aloud, reaching over to the desk to take out her box of stationery. She pulled out a blank sheet and her favorite purple pen and began to write.

Dear Sam,

I tried to see you this past Sunday at Figaro's, but you were out delivering pizza. Poor Sam. You work so hard!

Remember when I told you that Amy was auditioning for a rock band? It turned out to be Emmett and the Heartbreak. Emmett really liked Amy's voice and she has a second audition. I have a problem though and I hope you can help.

Shanon and Max think it's great that Amy is really into this guy Emmett, but I don't. Do you know him? Or have you heard about him? Is there anything you can tell me about him? Is he as cool as everyone else thinks he is?

Palmer

P.S. There will be a Valentine's Day Dance. I hope you can come. I'll let you know details soon.

P.P.S. You never told me your thoughts on valentines.

CHAPTER EIGHT

———◆———

Dear Lisa,

Sorry to hear you're bored. I have too much English homework to do to think about being bored.

Amy auditioned for this rock band. This cool guy Emmett is the leader and he's older than all of us and a real professional. Palmer thinks Emmett's weird and not a good guy, but Max and I agree with Amy that this is one of the best things that has ever happened to a Fox. I'm sure Amy'll write you about it. Since the audition though, she and Palmer have been sort of feuding, but I think everything will work out.

I was glad to hear about the new girl in your class. And also slightly jealous just because I miss you and wish we were still at the same school together.

I guess I should get back to work on my French and math. I've been ignoring them since I started the paper-that-wouldn't-end.

Love,
Shanon

Dear Mighty Mars,

To answer your question—I'm not quite sure how Max feels about Paul, but I think they have a lot in common. Paul hates girls and Max hates boys. So, that might be the beginning of a wonderful relationship—or a horrible one! They would have so much to talk about—what they don't like about the opposite sex.

How's your February going? Is it as cold at Ardsley as it is at Alma?

My paper is going. It's pages long and I'm still not near the end. Maybe I should have done the assignment and forgotten how I feel, like Palmer suggested. But I like it; it's fun to write. I just hope Mr. Griffith likes it. I had to get another extension. I'm on page twenty-five and I'm still not done. I'm handing it in next Wednesday whether it's finished or not.

> *Freezing in February,*
> *Shanon*

"Amy's right about February," Max complained, wrapping her multicolored scarf around so that it covered her nose and mouth. "It's freezing!"

"It could be worse," Shanon said, glancing at her roommate as they stepped carefully on the icy sidewalk toward Booth Hall.

"What could possibly be worse than gray days, below-zero weather, and a French quiz?"

"Two French quizzes?" Shanon suggested.

"Oh, you!" Maxie exclaimed, pushing Shanon so she skidded on the ice. "Race you to the mailboxes!"

The two girls slipped and slid the rest of the way and arrived at Booth Hall, laughing and out of breath.

"Look, a letter from Jose!" Max crowed.

"Read it out loud," Shanon pleaded. "It will make up for the fact that I didn't get one."

Dear Maxie,

I don't understand. Why shouldn't I like girls? Girls are just as good as boys, sometimes better. Like the girl who sits in front of me in school. Her name is Hilary and she has this long, long braid that sometimes falls on my desk when she turns her head. I'm going to give her a secret valentine. I don't know if it will be candy or a ribbon for her braid. What do you think? I hope she likes me or will like me after I give her the secret valentine.

I am practicing my spelling. See, I spelled shouldn't right. And I know three other words.

adobe—a sun-dried brick
pioneer—someone who first enters an area
spectator—a person who watches something
Aren't they grate words?

Love,
Jose

P.S. How come you hate boys?

"I don't hate boys. How can he say that?" Maxie wailed.

"You don't hate boys?" Shanon asked.

"No!" Maxie insisted. *I just don't know how to talk to them,* she thought to herself. "Jose is just saying that because of how I answered his letter. He seems a little young to be having a girlfriend."

"Max, I have to tell you something," Shanon stammered, her face red.

"What?" Max felt distracted. Jose's letter really both-

52

ered her. She didn't want people to think she hated boys; they just scared her and made her feel too tall, too awkward, and too strange.

"I thought you hated boys too when you didn't want to invite anyone to the dance. Also, you don't like talking about them, so I told Mars that when he asked me if you would be interested in Paul Grant."

"Shanon, how could you!" Max knew she was turning splotchy red, which always happened when she blushed. She couldn't even blush prettily. "I just didn't want to ask anyone to *this* dance! Is that so horrible? Is that a crime? Why is that so unusual?"

"I'm sorry, Maxie," Shanon protested, twisting her scarf in her hands.

"You write back to Mars that I do not hate boys! It's just so embarrassing that Mars and the other guys are always pushing me and Paul together. Imagine how you would feel if you were being thrown at some guy by his friends. I feel stupid—like I'm not even a real person. And I bet Paul doesn't even like me by now; he must be sick of my name and he barely even knows me. Your friend Mars is ruining my chance of Paul and me becoming friends."

"Maxie—"

"That isn't all," Maxie spoke over Shanon's tentative reply. "Paul and I never have a chance to get to know each other because there are like six people waiting to see if we like each other. I mean, really, Shanon, how can we talk to each other comfortably when there are twelve eyeballs staring at us all the time?"

"Well, that wasn't all I wrote," Shanon said more loudly, not looking Max in the eye. "When Mars asked me what you thought of Paul Grant, I joked in the letter that you and he have a lot in common. He hates girls and you hate boys."

"Paul hates girls?" Maxie asked slowly. Suddenly her stomach, which just had butterflies, now felt as though a lead weight were resting there.

"Max?" Shanon asked, not sure where her roommate's thoughts were taking her.

"Well, if he hates girls, that's fine. Let him and Mars think what they like. I couldn't care less!"

"Max, are you all right?" Shanon asked, worried.

"I'm perfectly perfect. I'm just going to answer this letter to Jose right away. I'll see you later, Shanon." Max turned quickly away, her face bright red.

Dear Jose,

I don't hate anyone. Really. I don't like everyone, but I don't hate all girls or all boys. I didn't mean to write a letter that made you think that. You know I don't hate you. You're one of my most favorite people.

I'm glad you like Hilary. She sounds very pretty. Is she nice, too? You know, you don't have to give her a present to make her like you. She either likes you or she doesn't. She'll probably like you best if you just be yourself around her. Let her know the Jose I know.

Congratulations (another big word) on your spelling. The definitions were great! I'm so proud of you. You seem to be working very hard. If I learn any new words that I really like, I'll let you know.

Good luck with Hilary and let me know what happens.

Love,
Maxie

Dear Palmer,

I think valentines are all right, but I don't like being told when to tell someone I like how I feel. I believe in letting someone know when the feeling hits me. So, on principle, I don't send them out.

I know Emmett, but I prefer not to say anything about him. I don't like to badmouth the competition. I wish Amy luck in whatever happens.

Got to go study, study, study.

Best,
Sam

CHAPTER NINE

Amy knew exactly what the poets meant by a singing heart. As she bicycled to town on Thursday, she could feel her heart singing with joy. Of course, her heart was singing a rock song, not some sappy love song. Her entire body felt happy. She was going for her second audition with Emmett. He must have thought she was pretty good if he would want to spend more time on her.

She turned right on his street and locked her bike. Her stomach suddenly felt like a mass of Jell-O, all quivery. No matter how brave a front she put on before her suitemates, she was still scared about auditioning and being with an older guy.

Emmett's aunt answered the door after Amy knocked loudly three or four times. "Oh, hello, dear, you must be here to see Emmett. He's downstairs, and when he's working, he doesn't like to be disturbed by such things as answering the door. It might interrupt his creative flow." His aunt continued to explain as she walked back into the kitchen, leaving Amy to find her way downstairs.

Amy quietly crept down the stairs, not wanting to bother

Emmett in case he was in the middle of some creative thinking, but when she finally got to the bottom of the stairs, she saw he was lying on the couch with his feet up, reading a comic book.

"A-hem." Amy coughed softly. "A-hem!" She coughed with a little more force. "Excuse me, Emmett, I'm here," she finally said loudly.

Slowly he put the comic book down and peered over at her.

"You're a—" He hesitated.

"Amy Ho. You asked me to come back today for my second audition," she prompted him.

"Oh, yeah, right." Amy almost giggled when she noticed his hair, for it was clean today. She noticed it was slightly wavy with red highlights. He was wearing ripped jeans, a work shirt, and a dirty T-shirt. Palmer would just hate his clothes. Amy thought they were great.

"Where is the rest of the band?" Amy asked tentatively as she took off her coat.

"Oh, I don't need them for the second audition. I'm the one who decides who joins my band and who doesn't."

"Oh. Are other girls coming?"

"Nah. Just you." He stared at her intently.

Amy felt a little strange being down in the basement alone with Emmett when she thought there would be the same sort of crowd as on Sunday. *Well, that's show biz,* she thought to herself.

"What would you like me to do?" she asked after a few moments of silence.

"Sing that song of yours, 'Cabin Fever.' I'm going to tape it, so I can listen to it when you leave and get more of a chance to listen to your voice, okay?"

"Sure," Amy said nervously. She was used to singing with her guitar, but she wasn't going to let the lack of an instrument stop her. She sang the song for him twice and at the end of the second time, he clapped loudly and smiled for the first time.

"Great, kid! You have a wonderful voice. A real natural rock and roll singing voice."

"I do?"

"Yeah, if I were you I wouldn't let anyone get near that voice with lessons or anything. It would ruin it."

"Ruin it?" Amy immediately thought of the private lessons she had with Professor Bernard. "But Professor Bernard at Alma Stephens has been coaching me. He's in favor of lessons and training."

"Of course he is. But how old is he? He belongs to the old school. You ask anyone else—anyone who understands the voice and rock—and they'll tell you not to mess with your voice. You want to feel how to sing, not control it."

"Sort of like when you told me to dance when I sang!" Amy suggested.

"Yeah! You know it, Amy baby. I knew you were a natural the moment I saw you. You have a rare talent and lessons will just cover it up!" Emmett grinned at her, pushing his hair out of his face. "You know, you stick with me, I can show you all the ropes."

"You mean I have the job?" Amy asked, her voice squeaking.

"No, no, kid, I didn't mean that just yet. I have to listen to your tape. I need the perfect combo of lead singer and new guitarist to get this show on the road again. But you're definitely up there. A special talent. You have the look of a rocker." He stared at her for a few moments and walked around her, tapping his finger against his lips. "Hmm, with the right clothes that *I* would pick out, of course, and some heavy makeup, you would be perfect. What's your schedule like?"

"I go to school every day," Amy began, worried since her parents didn't allow her to wear makeup.

"We all do, kid. Of course, I'm a straight-A student at Brighton High."

"You lead a band and you get straight A's. Wow! How do you do that?"

"You're not the only one around here who has a touch of genius." He smiled, looking straight into her eyes. He put his arm around her and led her over to a full-length mirror. "Look at us together—we make a great-looking couple, don't we?"

Amy swallowed nervously and stared into the mirror. Slowly she grinned; Emmett was right. He was tall and slender, casual yet graceful. He seemed to do everything in slow motion while she seemed to have enough energy crackling out of her whole body for the two of them. "Yeah, we do look good together."

"You know, being in a band means working a lot together, getting to know each other inside and out," Emmett said softly, taking her hands in his. Amy just nodded blankly. "You think you're up for that?"

"Y-yes."

"So do I." He leaned over and kissed her on her eyelids. "You and me—we could be something special." He smiled at her slowly and let go of her hands. "So, can you work nights? My band is real popular and we have some heavy gigs coming up."

"Sure," Amy answered in a daze. "I guess," she added,

once she actually heard his question, not worrying about how she could swing getting Miss Pryn to let her play in the band.

"So, let me tape you singing this song one more time and this time, let it go. Dance, scream it, do whatever you want, whenever it hits you."

Amy grinned at Emmett and jumped on the table, singing "Cabin Fever" for the thousands of people she imagined would be listening—and for him.

"And then, when I finished singing 'Cabin Fever' for the last time, he whistled and clapped. He told me again that with my looks, energy, and voice, I was the most extraordinary girl he had ever met," Amy babbled as soon as she was back in the suite. Maxie had made hot chocolate and the three girls listened as they all sipped their drinks. Shanon stared at Amy, wide-eyed. She never had a friend before who could possibly be a rock and roll star.

"Way to go, Ho!" Maxie shouted, giving Amy a high five.

"This is the coolest, Amy. I knew you were great, but I don't know anything about music," Shanon began, grinning. "But when a real rocker tells you this, then you know you're incredible. You should write Lisa all about it."

"It sounds as if he likes you," Maxie teased.

"I don't think so," Amy answered, not telling her suitemates that he had held her hand, kissed her, or what he had said. "It's all business, but there is something there. It's just the connection two artists have when they're really in synch with each other. I really like being with him. He makes me feel alive."

Palmer opened her mouth to interrupt and tell Amy what

Sam said in his letter, but she kept quiet. Sam only hinted that there was something wrong with Emmett. She still didn't have hard proof to show Amy that she was right. She'd just have to wait.

"Anyway, I have to go," Amy continued, getting her down jacket from her room.

"Going to Kringle's lesson?" Shanon asked.

"No," Amy answered. "I'm skipping it. Like Emmett says, I need to be alone to get in touch with my true genius. A lesson with Professor Bernard would just confuse me." With that answer Amy walked out of the suite, letting the door close behind her.

" 'In touch with her true genius'?" Shanon asked the other two after a moment of shocked silence. "What's that mean?"

"I've never heard that before. Even my father doesn't talk that way," Maxie said.

"Why didn't Emmett tell Amy if she was one of the semifinalists at least? Or whatever they call them. She's seen him twice." Shanon turned to Max. "Is that normal in show business?"

"I don't know, but this definitely isn't show business. It's just a local rock band. And Emmett's still a teenager even if he is older than we are. I think she likes him," Max reflected.

"Maybe," Shanon said. "Doesn't it seem like he's stringing her along though?" Max nodded her answer. "She's always loved her lessons with Kringle even if she did get frustrated. Under Emmett's influence, she's doing things she never did before."

"She'll definitely be disappointed if she doesn't get to sing with Emmett," Max added.

"Let's just keep our fingers crossed," Shanon suggested.

Dear Sam,

You're the only one I can talk to about any of this and I can't really tell you what is happening. All I can say is please, please, please tell me what you know about Emmett and the Heartbreak (especially Emmett). Amy's been hanging out with Emmett or at least she's seen him twice and really wants to be part of that band. She thinks Emmett is perfect. Is he? I won't bother you about this again if you just tell me what you know and think. She's changed ever since she met him.

On a much happier note, there will definitely be a Valentine's Day Dance . . . on Valentine's Day, next Saturday night. Instead of a band, there will be a deejay playing tapes (there wasn't enough money for a band). I hope you can come.

I hope everything is going well with you.

Palmer

P.S. I liked your idea of sending cards and stuff whenever you wanted to instead of just doing it once a year. But I also think that getting a valentine card makes the day special and personal—especially if it's from someone you care about.

Dear Mars,

Everything is topsy-turvy in the suite. Is it my imagination or was last year calmer?

Anyway, there will be a Valentine's Day Dance here at

Alma on the fourteenth (next Saturday night). I hope you can come.

Don't say anything, but I know Max isn't inviting Paul Grant, but the good news is that she isn't inviting anyone else either. I don't really know what she thinks of him, but I don't think you should keep pushing them together or at least not so obviously.

I have no idea what Amy is doing.

I hope everything is right-side-up in your suite. We need someone to give this suite a good shake and put everything back to normal.

I hope to see you on the fourteenth!

> *All shook up,*
> *Shanon*

P.S. How are the workouts going?

CHAPTER TEN

"Ms. Ho, is that you?" Amy groaned; it was Professor Bernard. She was standing at the pay phone outside the school dining hall, deciding whether or not to call Emmett and see if he had made a decision. It was Monday, over a week since the first audition and days since her private audition and still no word. She was miserable. "Ms. Ho, you not only don't show up for your lessons, but you don't answer me when I speak to you?"

"I'm sorry, Professor Bernard, I was thinking," Amy apologized, turning to face her incredibly tall teacher.

"Have you been thinking since Thursday when you missed our lesson and this morning when you missed another one? Have you been thinking so much you don't even tell me you need to cancel?"

"No . . . I mean yes . . . I'm sorry," Amy began, feeling her face turn pink.

"Why have you not shown up or contacted me? Have you been sick?"

"No."

"Too much other schoolwork?"

"No."

"Something the matter with your family?" he asked softly.

"No."

"Then what, Ms. Ho?"

"I—I just don't think I need to have lessons anymore," Amy explained, taking a deep breath. "I'm sorry I haven't contacted you; that was very rude."

"You are right: you've been very rude, but we will put that matter aside. I am more interested in why you don't think you need lessons anymore."

"I—I . . ." Amy began, unsure as to how to explain. "Well, it's like this. A professional musician told me that I have this amazing natural talent and voice, and that lessons would just ruin it. And I don't want to ruin my voice or my musical genius."

"This 'professional' told you that you were a musical genius."

"Yes."

"I see." He paused for so long that Amy was sure he understood and agreed. She smiled at him. "That is the biggest piece of nonsense I have heard in all my years as a teacher. Mozart was a musical genius. Beethoven was a musical genius. But Amy Ho is *not* a musical genius!" he thundered. "You are good, very good, but that is all you are right now. And you will never get any better without hard work and dedication. If you want to be more than a two-bit singer, you will have to work hard, study a lot, rehearse, and train. And now, listening to this, I don't know if you can do this. I am not even sure I would want you as my student."

"But, Professor Bernard . . ."

"I have heard enough! You have upset me very much."

"But . . ." Amy started.

"I don't want to speak with you anymore about this right now. Come on Thursday when you usually have your lesson and we will talk then. I need time to cool down and you need time to think—really think." Professor Bernard looked at her sternly and then walked away, shaking his head and muttering.

Knowing the only way to shake off her frustration and anger would be to run it off, Amy headed for the indoor track in the gym. She knew the path was usually empty in the late afternoon, so she was sure no one would bother her.

"Hey, Amy, wait up!" Max called from behind.

"What?" Amy looked around. "Oh, hi, sorry, Max."

"I'm going to the gym to swim. What's going on?" Max asked casually. Her usually energetic suitemate seemed very low.

"Oh, nothing much. Palmer's being more of a pain than usual; I just had a horrible fight with my voice teacher, and I still don't know if I'm part of the Heartbreak yet! Outside of that, everything is just peachy!" Amy finished, trying to laugh. The girls went off the path and tromped through the snow.

"February is not your month, is it?" Max joked weakly. "What happened with you and Kringle? Was he angry that you didn't show up for your lesson last Thursday?"

"Last Thursday and this morning," Amy confessed. "He also said that I'm not a musical genius and he isn't sure that he wants to work with me anymore. Now that he doesn't want me as a student, I don't want to give up the lessons. I was really learning a lot. I don't know what I

66

want or what's going on. I want to be in the band with Emmett, keep taking lessons with Kringle, get back to being friends with Palmer, and get out of February feeling good."

"Maybe you can talk with Kringle for starters."

"He told me to come in on Thursday and talk. He was too angry now. I've never had a teacher angry at me before in my life. It's awful!"

"Well, it sounds good that he wants to talk with you. I can't help you with Palmer; only you can do that, but I am sorry you haven't heard from Emmett yet."

"I just wish I would hear from him one way or another. I was about to call him when Professor Bernard came up, but I want to talk with Emmett in person, not on the phone. Maybe if he doesn't want me as part of the band, I could jam with him or them on Saturdays."

"Why don't you write to him and ask him about it?"

"Write to him?"

"Sure. Isn't that what our suite is famous for?"

"Yeah," Amy agreed, brightening. "But I prefer to ask him to jam in person." Amy thought to herself as they walked nearer the gym. "You know, you gave me a great idea. I can write him a letter, asking him to the Valentine's Day Dance, and I can talk to him about what's going on then."

"Invite him to the dance? What about John?"

"This is too good to pass up. Seeing Emmett is the most important thing in the world right now," Amy insisted, smiling again.

"Do you have a crush on him or something, Amy?" Maxie asked. "It's okay if you do, but he's kind of old."

"No, silly, I don't have a crush on him," Amy insisted

strongly. Why was everyone asking her that? She didn't think she really liked him—or did she? "Romance has nothing to do with my musical career. This is more important than romance. Emmett is the first person who ever told me I could make it as a rock star. He's going to help me make my dreams come true."

"Yeah, but . . ."

"Max, don't you understand?" Amy asked, her eyes bright. "You, of all people, should understand because of your dad. Emmett's the only person who has ever told me that I have genius and I'm not going to let that go!"

CHAPTER ELEVEN

"Amy, I don't understand why you're not inviting John," Shanon said Monday night, sitting in her room with her suitemate.

"Because I need to see Emmett to discuss my future with him," Amy explained, spreading out on Maxie's bed and getting ready to write her letter.

"Yes, but . . ."

"John won't care," Amy assured her. "He can come to the dance if he wants. He doesn't need my invitation."

"You're not even going to write to explain it to him?"

"Shanon, there's nothing to explain. We're not going together; I don't owe him anything."

"I just wish everything was back to normal," Shanon mumbled under her breath.

"Anyway, it will be cool to be there with Emmett," Amy sighed, thinking of his holding her hands and saying they looked great as a couple. "And you'll get to meet him and see what a great guy he really is. He's real different from the way he seemed the day of the auditions."

"Mail call!" Maxie shouted, entering the suite.

"Anything for me?" Palmer asked.

"Hmm, no nothing, sorry, Palmer," Max answered. "I have two letters for Shanon and one for me. Do you want to come in while I read my letter?"

"No," Palmer snapped. She had been sitting at her desk, just staring at her math homework. Without Amy to help her, she had been struggling for the last week through all her assignments. "I have to work on my math."

"Call if you need help," Max offered as she entered her room.

"Do you mind if I use your bed for letter writing, Max? I can think better in here."

"It's okay, Amy," Maxie said, looking at Shanon who rolled her eyes. "I'll share Shanon's bed for reading my letter. I wonder who it's from; it doesn't have a name on the outside—or a return address."

"It's a red envelope; maybe it's a valentine," Amy teased.

"Mine is from Mars. I hope he's coming to the dance," Shanon said, wriggling over on the bed to make room for Max. She looked at the other one and noticed that it said "Confidential—do not read aloud."

Dear Shanon,

I would be delighted to honor your school with my presence on the evening of St. Valentine's Day. I would also consider it a dream-come-true if we were to meet and dance together.

How do you like that response, Shanon? I'm practicing being a gentleman. Can't wait to see you on the fourteenth.

Counting the hours,
Mars
P.S. Paul Grant is going to the dance, but he's going with-

out a date. As you probably know, I'm shocked that he's going at all since he hates women. Will wonders never cease?

P.P.S. How's your English paper going? Did you hand it in? Did you get it back? What's the scoop?

P.P.P.S. You will not recognize me—my muscles are bulging everywhere. I hope I can fit through the gym doors.

"Mars is going to the dance! Hurray!"

"Shh, I'm trying to write this letter to Emmett," Amy said.

Dear Emmett,

I'm sure you'll be a little surprised to get this letter.

I would like to invite you to the Alma Stephens Valentine's Day Dance, which will be on February fourteenth. I just want to talk to you about what is happening with the band, if you decided who your lead singer will be, and other business. The dance will be the easiest place to talk. You could probably also talk to the head of the social committee and book some gigs that very night.

I hope to see you this Saturday.

Sincerely yours,
Amy Ho

Dear Shanon,

Hi, I hope this isn't too strange, getting a letter from me, but you're the only one I can talk to about this. If you can, be at The Ledger office at seven-thirty, Tuesday morning. I must speak to you privately. I'll be there Wednesday morning also if I don't hear from you on Tuesday. Thanks.

John Adams

Shanon looked up, but Amy was totally involved in her writing and Max was reading her letter. Shanon slipped John's letter under her pillow and picked up the one from Mars, pretending to read it again.

Dear Max,

I hope you'll be my valentine. I've only seen you from afar and hope we can get closer. See you at the dance.

Your mystery valentine,
PG

"I got a valentine!" Max exclaimed, waving the card over her head.

"From whom?" Shanon asked, leaning over to look.

"I don't know. It's signed PG."

"This is so neat," Shanon squeaked. "I bet it's from Paul Grant."

"Just because it's signed PG?"

"Who else do you know with those initials who lives in Brighton? See, it has the Brighton post-office seal on the envelope."

"You're right about that," Maxie mused.

"I bet he likes you," Shanon told her.

"I don't know."

"Come on. He sends you a valentine letter, saying he'll see you at the dance. You can't say The Unknown made him do this. No one can make someone write something."

"I guess you're right."

"Come on, Maxie," Amy said, "be positive. He wouldn't have said what he did if he didn't mean it."

"Yeah, but I thought he hated girls."

"You know," Shanon offered, "just because he tells the

guys that he hates girls doesn't mean he really does. I mean guys don't always tell their friends everything or even the truth. I bet some of the things Mars tells me he wouldn't ever tell his friends—he'd be afraid they'd think he was wimpy."

"That makes sense," Maxie agreed. She looked down at the card and read it again.

"It's so romantic," Shanon sighed.

"Yes, it is." Maxie smiled softly and slipped the card into her diary. She settled back on her bed and imagined meeting Paul at the dance.

CHAPTER TWELVE

—————◆—————

Shanon set her alarm for six-thirty on Tuesday morning. In the dark room she quickly and quietly got dressed so she wouldn't wake Maxie. Shivering in the cold, she hoped that whatever John needed to talk about was worth this. She also hoped that no one would catch her in *The Ledger* office using the computer for unofficial reasons.

Shanon silently locked the suite door and softly ran down the stairs and out of Fox Hall toward *The Ledger* office. At seven-fifteen the sun was just barely up. It felt as if everyone was still sleeping and Shanon almost thought that she had traveled across time; it could be one hundred years ago and she was trapped in an earlier age.

Almost as a response, she heard a truck backfire in the distance, reminding her that she was firmly in the twentieth century and that she was about to talk to John Adams by the computer.

She hurried along the last few yards and was enveloped by warm air as she entered the building that housed the school newspaper. Running up the stairs, she glanced at her watch. It was already seven-thirty. She was late!

She took out the keys to the office and hoped that Kate would not decide to come to the newspaper early this morning. Kate just wouldn't understand breaking the rules, and Shanon wasn't too sure she had a good excuse this time. She didn't even know what John wanted.

She turned on one light by the computer and quickly flicked a couple of switches and watched the machine come to life. John was online already.

/SEN 99 ARDSLEY LIT. MAG. IDENTIFY YOURSELF./GA

OKAY. IT'S JOHN. YOU'RE LATE./GA

OKAY. SORRY. Shanon typed in frustration. She didn't need a scolding first thing on a freezing cold Tuesday morning. WHAT'S SO URGENT?/GA

OKAY. SORRY, TOO. I'VE JUST BEEN UPSET. I HAVEN'T HEARD FROM AMY IN THREE WEEKS AND I'VE SENT HER TWO LETTERS. I DIDN'T KNOW WHO ELSE TO ASK. IS SHE OKAY?/GA

Shanon was stuck. She didn't know what to say to John. Amy was fine, but she was totally involved with Emmett, and it seemed as if no one else existed for her right now. How could she say that to John? And did she have any right to say anything to John? OKAY. AMY HAS BEEN VERY BUSY. I RARELY SEE HER./GA That answer seemed fairly noncommital to Shanon.

OKAY. DO YOU KNOW WHY SHE HASN'T WRITTEN ME? I'M SORRY TO BE ASKING YOU THESE QUESTIONS. I WOULD ASK AMY, BUT SINCE SHE ISN'T WRITING ME, IT'S SORT OF HARD. I WROTE HER A POEM THAT WAS SORT OF PERSONAL AND SHE DIDN'T EVEN ANSWER THAT ONE./GA

"This isn't fair," Shanon muttered aloud. She knew the poem that John meant. It spelled out Amy's name. She couldn't believe that Amy hadn't thought of John's feelings.

OKAY. I DON'T KNOW WHAT TO SAY. YOU HAVE TO TALK TO AMY ABOUT ALL THIS. I WOULD HELP IF I COULD, BUT THIS IS BETWEEN THE TWO OF YOU. SHE IS AWFULLY BUSY, BUT I'M SURE ONCE ALL THIS IS OVER, IT WILL BE LIKE OLD TIMES./GA

OKAY. ONCE WHAT IS OVER? I KNOW. I HAVE TO WAIT FOR AMY TO TELL ME. ISN'T THIS FAMILIAR, SHANON? JUST LIKE LAST YEAR WHEN I WANTED TO KNOW WHY PALMER WASN'T WRITING. I DON'T SEEM TO HAVE MUCH LUCK WITH PEN PALS./GA

OKAY. THAT'S NOT TRUE. YOU AND AMY ARE GREAT PEN PALS. THIS IS JUST NOT A GREAT MONTH. FEBRUARY BLUES, YOU KNOW./GA

OKAY. I'VE ALWAYS LIKED FEBRUARY UNTIL THIS YEAR. I HAVEN'T EVEN GOTTEN AN INVITATION TO THE VALENTINE'S DAY DANCE./GA

OKAY. I SHOULD GO. BYE, JOHN./GA

OKAY. BYE, SHANON./GA

Shanon hit a few more keys after they finished talking and shut the computer down. She looked around the office to make sure everything was all right and then turned off the light.

She felt horrible. She wasn't able to help John one bit and soon he would find out that Amy had asked another guy to the dance.

Shanon pushed the main doors open and stepped outside into the cold. The sun was definitely up and she even saw students and teachers tramping across the grounds. Everyone else looked so happy—everyone but the Foxes in Fox Hall.

"Shanon, is that you? You're up early." Shanon looked up and saw Ms. Grayson-Griffith's smiling face. She was walking Gracie. "What's wrong, dear?"

"Everything," Shanon blurted out, "and I don't know how to fix any of it."

"Can you tell me? No, don't jump, Gracie," she said, pulling on the dog's leash. "She's happy to see you."

Kneeling down on the cold ground, Shanon let Gracie lick her face, her warm tongue comforting her.

"I don't know. How can you help if I can't and they're all my friends?" she asked, still holding on to Gracie's wiggling body.

"Hmm, trouble in the suite?" Shanon nodded. "Are you involved in it?"

"I live there."

"I know, dear, but is it trouble between you and one of the other girls? Or does the problem have to do with some of the others in the suite?"

"No more, Gracie." Shanon stood up. "I guess the others. I don't feel like I can tell you the details because I'm not directly involved."

"Then I think you can just be a good friend by being there and listening, but you can't make it better all by yourself."

"But everything used to be great," Shanon protested. "If it can just go back to the way it was three weeks ago, everything would be fine."

Ms. Grayson-Griffith put her hand on Shanon's shoulder. "I know you don't want to hear this, but things change and part of growing up is accepting the change and moving on."

"But—"

"I know it doesn't seem fair. I used to always say that." Ms. Grayson-Griffith laughed. "My mother used to tell me exactly what I'm saying to you and I never wanted to hear it, but now I see she was right. I still don't like it, but I've learned to accept that some of the things and people I love change. All I can do is still love them and let them go." Ms. Grayson-Griffith tugged on the leash slightly. "One more thing, Shanon, since you say this doesn't involve you directly. You can't take care of other people's lives. You can suggest things or give advice, but you can't do things for them. They have to do it themselves. It's too early in the morning for all of this preaching. Come and talk to me whenever you need to—we'll do it inside next time."

"Thanks."

"How's your paper going? I hear it's an epic."

Shanon groaned. "I'm almost finished. I have to be—it's due tomorrow."

"Well, I know someone who is looking forward to reading it. See you in class later on, Shanon. Come on, Gracie, ten more minutes and then it's time to go in." Ms. Grayson-Griffith waved at Shanon and then continued on her way.

Shanon stared after her teacher, wishing she could have told her the whole story, but knowing it wasn't hers to tell.

"I don't care what she says, I still wish everything would stay the same," Shanon muttered to herself as she stomped through the snow back to the dorm.

CHAPTER THIRTEEN

———————◆———————

"Hey, Palmer!" Palmer turned around, hugging her books to her chest. The cold wind blew her blond hair into her face, blinding her temporarily. "It's me! Georgette!"

Palmer frowned. On this cold, blustery day, Georgette looked warm and happy. Her blond hair was tucked into her woolen turquoise cap; her face seemed rosy but not cold; and she was practically skipping down the slightly icy walk. "Hi, Georgette," Palmer answered flatly.

"Get up on the wrong side of the bed?" her sister teased, falling into step beside Palmer.

"No."

"Where are you going?"

"To Booth Hall."

"Oh, another pen pal letter. What are you wearing to the dance?"

"I don't know yet."

"How can you not know? It's Thursday—it's only three days away!"

"Oh, I'll put on some old thing," Palmer said, trying to

sound casual. "You know there's more to life than clothes and dances."

"What's Sam wearing?" Georgette pressed on.

"I don't know what Sam's wearing!" Palmer answered, annoyed. "What does it matter to you?"

"I just thought you might want to coordinate with him."

"Well, I don't know what he'll be wearing."

"Just ask him."

Palmer stopped and turned to look at her sister. "Look, I don't know why it's so important to you to know what I'm wearing or what Sam's wearing. You'll see at the dance, okay?"

"Isn't Sam going?"

"What made you ask that?" Palmer exclaimed.

Georgette took a step back. "I don't know, Palmer. It just doesn't seem like you not to know all the important details like what Sam's wearing or which dress you'll choose, so I thought perhaps you were keeping something from me."

Palmer peered at her sister, thinking hard. "Well, to tell you the truth, I haven't heard from Sam yet, but I know he's going to the dance. He just hasn't had time to write me yet."

"I'm sure you'll get a letter today, Palmer. How could he not want to go with you?"

"Of course he wants to go with me! He just hasn't formally told me so yet. That's why I'm going to the mailbox now. I'm sure there will be a letter," Palmer answered, beginning to walk toward Booth Hall again.

"Well, if you want to borrow anything, just come on over." Georgette waved as she took the path back toward her dorm. Without realizing it, Palmer smiled. It might not be so bad having a sister here, she thought to herself, even if it is Georgette.

As she approached the mailbox, she realized that she wanted a letter to be there today! *No more waiting around,* she thought. What if Sam still hadn't answered? What if he didn't want to go to the dance? She couldn't imagine what was taking him so long. Didn't he know the dance was only three days away?

Taking a deep breath, she opened the box and pulled out a letter—it was for her—from Sam! It felt better than usual! Without waiting to get back to her room, she tore the envelope open.

Dear Palmer,

I bet you've been wondering why I've taken so long to write to you. Your letter has been a hard one to answer. I don't like talking about people, especially when I don't have anything nice to say, but Amy is a friend of yours and I think you should know the truth. Especially with what I heard this past weekend, but more on that later.

I don't know Emmett real well, especially since he's older and dropped out of Brighton High. He used to get into a lot of trouble at school and maybe he thought it wasn't worth getting suspended all the time.

Anyway, I've heard him play and he definitely has talent, but he's a very weird and difficult person. His bands are always breaking up. From what I hear from other musicians—guys who have been in his bands—he has a terrible temper and a fat ego. The music suffers because of his personality, so most people don't ever rehire him.

I know he's making—or trying to make—a comeback because of the auditions and because I saw him and his band this past weekend with a new female singer and guitarist at a competition in Springville.

This is the really sleazy part—he and the band were doing a special arrangement of "Cabin Fever." I remember John and Amy wrote a song by that title, so I went up to Emmett and asked him about it. And he said he wrote the song! He lied!

I guess you should warn Amy about him. I know it will be difficult. I think a lot of new people, who don't know Emmett, are usually taken in by his cool rock act. He has a real following.

Maybe you should try to get a second opinion. It would be a good idea to talk to someone who really knows him and likes him. He does have a group that follows him around, but I don't really like those people.

Anyway, to answer your second question—I wouldn't miss the Valentine's Day Dance for anything. I'm real glad they have a deejay so I can be at the dance with you.

I just reread this letter, and I hate to say it but I think you should tell Amy to stay away from Emmett and his band. Not only do they have a bad rep, which might rub off on her, but they're just not good guys.

See you in a few days!

Sam

Palmer felt so relieved. She was going to the dance! Sam still liked her! And he confirmed how she felt about Emmett. She was right all along—Emmett was definitely bad news and now she had proof!

Palmer stuffed the letter in her notebook and ran as fast she could back to Fox Hall, determined to get Amy to listen to her. Before she made the turn that led up to the front entrance, she heard a dog barking.

"Oh, Dan must be walking Gracie," she murmured to herself, turning the last corner. Then she stopped suddenly. There, standing next to Mr. Griffith, was Emmett—the creep himself!

CHAPTER FOURTEEN

Palmer quickly ducked behind a bush, close enough so she could overhear their conversation.

I can't believe I'm doing this, Palmer said to herself. *Me, Palmer Durand, hiding behind a bush. No one would believe it.*

"Stop, Gracie," she heard Dan say. Palmer hoped that Gracie couldn't smell her. The last thing she wanted was to be caught crouching behind a bush eavesdropping. It would be too humiliating.

"Now, what were you saying?" Dan addressed Emmett.

"Like I said, I need to see Amy Ho and I know she lives in this building," Emmett answered.

Palmer peered through the bush; she had never seen Dan Griffith so stern before. She wouldn't want to be in Emmett's shoes right now.

"If you know Amy lives here, you must be aware of some of our rules. Unplanned visits from boys are not allowed."

"Amy knows me, man. I just need to talk with her, you know. She sent me this note," Emmett said, pulling out Amy's letter from inside his jacket.

"Whether she knows you or not," Dan Griffith repeated, looking at Emmett in disbelief, "you cannot be on campus without special permission. I suggest you leave right now."

"You are living in the dark ages," Emmett sneered as he stuffed the letter into his back pants pocket. But, for all his bluster, Palmer could tell he was going to listen to Dan.

Palmer could see Mr. Griffith pointing the way out. If Emmett followed his direction, he would pass right by her. Watching Emmett saunter toward her, Palmer could see he had a smirk on his face. She peered through the bushes again and saw Mr. Griffith watch Emmett for a moment and then continue on his walk in the opposite direction.

"Hey," Palmer said, standing just as Emmett came closer.

"Yeah?" Emmett stopped short. She noticed that once again his hair was dirty, the knees in his jeans were ripped, and his sneakers were practically falling apart.

"Who are you looking for?" she asked boldly, although she felt her heart beating rapidly.

"What's it to you?" He looked at her, his eyes narrowing. "I'm looking for Amy. Hey, you're one of the girls who came with her, aren't you? I remember your hair. Yeah"—he smiled at her—"you're the real pretty one. Go get her for me, okay?" His voice had changed from rough to wheedling once he recognized Palmer.

Palmer just looked at him. Now that they were talking, she didn't know what to say or do. She wasn't even sure why she stopped him. "I know you. You're Emmett. And listen, you're wasting your time here, because Amy doesn't want to see you ever again!" Palmer blurted out, surprising herself.

"Come on, kid, don't give me a hard time. That old man just chewed my ear off about stupid rules—"

" 'That old man'! Mr. Griffith isn't an old man! Why don't you just get out of here now!" Palmer exclaimed.

"You got it all wrong, kid. Amy will want to see me. I just lost my female lead singer and Amy is my top choice. We have a gig on Valentine's Day at Lulu's Diner and I want Amy to be there with us."

"Well, too bad. Amy wouldn't want to sing with your band," Palmer persisted, flipping her hair back and looking above his head. She knew from practice that looking above someone's head just drove the other person crazy. "She told me all about singing with you and she thinks you and the Heartbreak are awful. She would never want to be in your band."

"Yeah, then why did she send me this letter asking me to come to this dumb dance?" Emmett demanded, pulling out Amy's letter again. He moved his head, trying to catch her eye.

"I have no idea. But I do know that she has no interest in you or your so-called band!"

"Is that so?" he asked, putting his hands on his hips, moving closer to Palmer and forcing her to look up at him.

Palmer stood her ground and wouldn't move backward. She was beginning to enjoy this conversation with Emmett—she felt as if she had him on the run.

"You want to get rejected twice? Why do you need to see Amy just to be told that she doesn't ever want to see you or play music with you again?"

"Forget it! This is more trouble than it's worth." Emmett threw his arms up in disgust. "I don't need you or your little friend." He turned to go, but then he faced

Palmer again. "You can tell your little friend that *you* just blew *her* chances of ever singing with me. I wouldn't want her in my band if *she* paid *me!*"

Palmer watched and waited until she could no longer see Emmett and she let out a big sigh of relief. She smiled triumphantly and strolled into Fox Hall, congratulating herself on a job well done. She ran up the stairs to her suite; she couldn't wait to tell the other Foxes the news.

When she got to the suite door, she stopped for a moment and tried to get the smile off her face. Although she was thrilled that she was right about Emmett and had just handled him perfectly, she realized that Amy might not see everything in the same light. She opened the door and ran into the suite. There she saw Amy, Max, and Shanon studying. They all looked up as she burst into the room. Shanon stood up and came toward her.

"Palmer, what is it?"

"I . . ." Palmer started.

"Is something wrong?" Even Amy looked concerned.

"I don't know how to begin. . . ."

"Just begin at the beginning." Amy moved closer to her roommate.

"I just had a fight with Emmett!" Palmer exclaimed.

"You had a fight with Emmett!" Amy repeated, pulling her arm away from Palmer. "Is he here?"

"Take off your coat, Palmer," Max coaxed.

"What happened?" Shanon asked, all three girls speaking at the same time.

Finally, Palmer took her coat off and sat on the loveseat, with the other three girls around her. Amy was next to her, Shanon sat on the floor, and Max pulled a chair closer. "He's horrible!" Palmer spit out.

"Yes, we've heard that before," Amy said, shaking Palmer slightly. "And he doesn't wash his hair. But what did he say? What kind of fight? Did he want to see me? Was he actually here at Alma Stephens?"

"Yes, yes!"

"What do you mean? He wants to see me and he's here, on campus?" Amy exclaimed, jumping up. "I have to go down and see him right away!"

"He's gone now. I was right about him all along so I sent him away. Wait till you hear what he did! I told him you don't ever want anything to do with him. You'll never have to talk to him again, that creep," Palmer explained.

"What!" Amy shouted. "You sent him away? How could you, Palmer Durand? I knew you were weird on the subject of Emmett, but I didn't think you'd go that far!" Even Max and Shanon were shocked.

"No, no, you don't understand, Amy. I did it for you and *because* he's such a creep," Palmer protested. This was not quite going the way she had imagined.

"Right, because he doesn't wash his hair!" Amy said disgustedly.

"No!"

"Amy, why don't you let Palmer explain," Shanon suggested, trying to speak calmly. She felt miserable—instead of getting better, things were just getting worse with each day. She started to wish that Maxie had never seen that ad in the paper. "Why don't you start at the beginning, Palmer?"

"I'm listening, but just barely," Amy said, sitting down again. "You'd better have some good answers. Why was he here and why did he want to see me? And what kind of fight?"

"He wanted you to sing with the band on Valentine's Day at Lulu's Diner," Palmer mumbled, not meeting Amy's eyes.

"And you sent him away? How could you? This could have been my big break! Lulu's is a really hot place!"

"Palmer!" Even Shanon was shocked. "You knew she wanted to sing with Emmett more than anything else in the world."

"Here, read Sam's letter," Palmer said. As Amy read it, Palmer explained what was in the letter to Max and Shanon.

"He stole her song?" Shanon asked, her eyes wide.

"That's illegal!" Max declared. "My father probably knows some good lawyers."

"Wait a minute. We don't know that he stole it. Maybe he was just giving me a chance to have my song out there so the public could hear it," Amy exclaimed hotly, after reading the letter twice through.

"Without giving you any credit and then lying about it?" Max asked.

"Maybe he thought it was none of Sam's business!" Amy declared.

"Maybe. But he shouldn't have lied. Amy, I'm sorry," Shanon said quietly, putting her arm around her suitemate's shoulders.

"Something is wrong here!" Amy announced, standing up suddenly. "You have no right to butt into my business, Palmer. I don't care what Sam wrote to you; he's wrong. And then you tell Emmett that I don't want to see him again! Just when he wanted me to sing with him. This ruins all my chances for ever being in his band."

"But, Amy, he stole your song. He lied to you about

being in high school," Max said, after skimming Sam's letter. "With everything he's done, I agree with Palmer. He's a creep. A double creep."

Amy stared at her suitemates in frustration. "You don't understand! I don't care what Sam's letter says. The main thing here is that you had no right to speak for me, Palmer. Because you did, I can never be part of his band," Amy stated quietly. "You should have showed me the letter and told me that Emmett was downstairs. It's my decision whether I sing with his band or not. Nobody makes decisions for me!"

"Obviously, Amy, you don't have one bone of gratitude in your body or you would be thanking me right now for helping you out."

"You make me so angry!" Amy practically shrieked.

"Look, it's all in black and white," Palmer said in a reasonable voice. "Sam has shown that—"

"I don't care what Sam thinks of Emmett as a musician. I think he is the most awesome musician I've ever heard. And he's the only one in this entire world who appreciates me and my singing!"

"I just stood up to this creep and saved you from being used by him and this is the thanks I get! That's the last time I ever try to help you out!" Palmer finally screamed back.

"I don't need this kind of help! My worst enemy couldn't have been more helpful."

"Great, Amy!" Palmer shouted. "You take everything I do and twist it to make me look bad. So before you say another word, let me just tell you what your perfect Emmett said before he left. Then you won't have to listen to me anymore. He said he never wants to see you again either!"

Amy said nothing for a moment. In the awful silence in the suite, Maxie heard a knock at the door. In a daze she answered it. It was Kate Majors, who walked right in. She had obviously just come in from outside. Her coat was still on, her hair was windblown, and she had only one boot on.

"What is going on in here? I could hear shouting from down the hall."

"It's nothing, Kate," Amy answered stiffly. "Palmer and I were having a little disagreement, but it won't happen again."

"That goes double for me," Palmer muttered.

Kate looked at the two girls and turned awkwardly to Shanon as she balanced on her bootless foot. "What is going on in this suite? You four girls are more trouble than the rest of the floor put together."

"N-nothing, Kate," Shanon stammered.

"If you all don't want to tell me, fine. But don't disturb the rest of the floor. If you do, I'll have to report you to Ms. Grayson and Mr. Griffith." Her duty done, Kate hobbled out of the suite, quietly closing the door behind her.

With the shutting of the door, Amy turned and went into her room. After a few moments she returned with her knapsack bulging and her pillow.

"Don't wait up for me. I'm going to stay in Brenda's room tonight." Before the other girls could utter a word, Amy walked out of the suite, leaving them in shocked silence.

CHAPTER FIFTEEN

"A little to the left, Shanon," Maxie directed. She stood on a ladder at one end of the dining hall, holding up a red streamer. On the far side of the room, Shanon also stood atop a ladder and was holding the rest of the roll and, with Maxie's help, was taping the streamer in the correct spot. "Perfect!"

"Great, just two more and then we'll put all the hearts up," Shanon called back. She climbed down the ladder and looked over at Amy who was sitting on the floor, leaning against the wall, and strumming her guitar softly. Amy was back sleeping in the suite at night, but she seemed very detached from everything that was going on around her.

"I could kill you for volunteering us to set up the decorations for the dance," Maxie complained to Shanon as they met in the center of the room where all the decorations were.

"I'm sorry, Max. I didn't realize it would be only the two of us actually doing the work. I expected Palmer to be here. I thought that when Kate said she was in charge of decorations that I should volunteer. She could easily have gone to Maggie or Dan about that horrible fight on Thursday night. You know she could have."

"I know."

"So this was a way to thank her, you know. I also thought that it might help get the Foxes back together, but I can see I was wrong about that." Shanon glanced at Amy again and then looked back at Max. "Palmer did say she would help, but. . . ."

"I just hope we have enough time to dress for tonight." Maxie was worried.

"Don't worry, we will." Shanon smiled, putting her hand on her roommate's shoulder. "You'll look beautiful for Paul tonight."

"Let's not get carried away. We'll settle for acceptable, passing, not disgusting."

Shanon laughed. "You're worse than I am. Trust me, you'll have fun."

"That's what you said about decorating. 'Trust me, we'll all work together and get along.' "

"Well, I have to be right about at least one thing this year."

"Let's finish the streamers." As Shanon moved the ladder, she heard the door to the dining hall open and close. She looked up and there was Palmer. Shanon sighed; Palmer definitely was dressed for the occasion. She had on red and white polka dot pants and a red and white top that *just* matched the balloons and streamers. However, putting up streamers seemed to be the last thing on her mind. Palmer looked around her and then purposely strode toward Amy. Amy glanced at Palmer and then looked back down at her guitar.

"Amy, we need to talk," Palmer started.

"Yes, I know." Amy strummed her guitar once as if to emphasize her agreement.

"I—"

"I—" Both girls started at the same time.

"I'll just say this quickly and then you can say whatever you want to," Palmer insisted.

"No, I need to go first," Amy went on, "because I want to just tell you—"

"Amy, let me just—"

"Palmer, I think you've done enough talking!" Amy said loudly, overriding her and standing up. She leaned the guitar against the wall. "I'm really angry at you and I've thought about this for days. You've done some pretty selfish things in the past, but nothing beats this one. You had no right to tell Emmett anything for me—I don't care what your motives were. No one has the right to make decisions for me. You blew my chances of performing with a rock band, and I can't forgive you for that."

"But I was right. Emmett is a creep! And you're too blind to see that! Obviously you've got a major 'thing' for him. You should be thanking me!"

"Thanking you?" Amy practically yelled. "I don't want to talk about this anymore. We have to live in the same room, but I don't have to talk to you. So I want you to stay on your side and I will stay on mine. I—I—" Amy's voice broke for a moment. "I don't think I want to be friends with you anymore."

"Well, that's fine with me!" Palmer exclaimed quickly, covering up her shocked feelings with anger. "The less I have to hear about your stuff, the better."

"Fine!" Amy declared, taking her guitar and moving toward another part of the dining hall.

"I came here to apologize," Palmer shouted at Amy's back. "But now I wouldn't apologize if you begged me on your knees. You deserve Emmett!"

She glared at Shanon and Max who just stared at her, with both of their mouths open.

"Palmer—" Shanon started.

"I don't want to hear anything right now, Shanon." Palmer quickly turned and walked straight out of the dining hall.

Shanon turned toward Amy and walked over to her. "Amy?"

"Well? What do you want?" Amy asked gruffly, trying to speak over the lump in her throat.

"Amy!" Shanon whispered. "Is it true? You don't want to be friends with Palmer?"

"Yes." Suddenly Amy couldn't look at her two suitemates.

"But, Amy, we're the Foxes," Shanon continued, not able to get her voice above a whisper.

"I know, Shanon," Amy stammered, sitting down on a hard chair, "but I just can't forgive her. Not this time. I'm too angry and hurt. And she stepped over the line; even my parents don't speak for me. We talk things over. Palmer went too far. All I can see when I look at her are all my chances disappearing."

"But she only did it to help you," Maxie finally said.

"But she *wasn't* helping me. She didn't think about my feelings. I've put up with a lot of Palmer's stuff and I know she wasn't looking out for me. She just wanted to show me that I was wrong about Emmett and she was right."

"But this is awful!" Shanon wailed. "I mean, our suite is always together. I've hated it these past couple of weeks

95

with you two disagreeing. I was sure that you could work it out."

"I'm tired of letting her get away with doing whatever she wants."

"Amy, come to the dance with us," Maxie offered, "and think about this more. Maybe in a few days you'll feel differently."

"No." Amy stood up. "I'm going to see Emmett. I'm going to tell him that Palmer spoke out of turn and if he wants me to be part of his band, then I will. You both will have to cover for me."

"But, Amy, it's six o'clock, dark, and icy out there. You don't have a pass," Maxie protested.

"Then I'll just sneak out. I have to let him know and talk to him in person. I'll bike to Lulu's—"

"But—" Shanon tried.

"I'm going," Amy said, cutting her off. "Are you going to help me?" Shanon nodded, feeling miserable.

"Be careful."

"I will," Amy promised.

"We'll tell them you decided you weren't feeling well and you're skipping the dance. But the moment you get back, you come to the dance so we know you're safe," Maxie insisted.

"I will. Don't worry. I'll be back in an hour or two at the most." Amy grinned, seeming like her old self. "Ciao!" With that, Amy practically danced out of the dining room.

The two roommates looked at each other, then went back to putting up the streamers and hanging the hearts on the wall, saying nothing more. Finally when they finished putting everything away, Maxie broke the silence. "I don't like this."

"Neither do I, but I don't think we have much of a choice right now. Nothing is turning out like we thought it would."

"I know."

"I'm really worried about Amy. Do you think she'll be okay?"

"I hope so." Maxie leaned the ladder against the wall. "Come on, we should hurry up, since we both have to take showers for tonight."

The two girls slowly put their coats on and turned out all the lights. They stepped outside into the cold darkness and could see their breaths as they exhaled.

"She'll be okay," Maxie said.

"Right!" Shanon whispered, crossing her fingers tightly as they headed back toward their dorm.

CHAPTER SIXTEEN

———◆———

"Any sign of her, Shanon?" Maxie asked, sitting on her bed.

"No," her roommate answered, standing at the window. "I can't see anything or anybody. Only a crazy person would be out on a bike in this weather."

"That's our Amy."

"And only two crazy people would let her." Shanon went back to her dresser and picked up her hairbrush. "Do you think we should go tell Dan and Maggie? It's been an hour and a half and still no Amy."

"She would be so angry . . ."

"Yes, but—"

"It's only eight o'clock now," Maxie answered, retying her bathrobe around her waist. "It takes an hour to bike into town and back even on the best of days. Besides, it will probably take some time to talk to Emmett. I'm sure she's fine."

"I don't want her to get hurt."

"I don't either."

"It's dark and icy out there."

"But Amy has to talk to Emmett and tell him that she really does want to play in his band. It's so important to her," Max reminded Shanon.

"I know. I guess we'll just wait another hour and if she doesn't come back by then, we'll tell Maggie and Dan. Two more hours at the most. If she gets caught, she'll get into a lot of trouble and so will we," Shanon mentioned lightly, although the very thought scared her. "And what are we going to do about the suite?"

"I don't know, Shanon. This is horrible with the two of them not talking to each other." Max opened the closet door to take out her dress when she heard a knock at the suite door. "I'll get it." Walking into the sitting room, she noticed that the door to the other bedroom was closed. Disappointed, she shook her head slightly. Palmer seemed to be freezing out Shanon and her along with Amy. Opening the front door, she was surprised to see Kate Majors in her bathrobe, holding a long, slender box. "Hi, Kate."

"Hi. Sorry to bother you, but I wanted to thank you for doing a great decorating job. You saved my life doing it. I've been working on a paper all day long and had no time to do it."

"It was fun," Max said, knowing Kate would never know she was being sarcastic.

"Oh, and this came for you. I don't know why it was delivered to my door."

"What is it?"

"I don't know. I don't open up packages that don't belong to me. See you at the dance." After Kate left, Max shut the door and returned to her room.

"Look what I got, Shanon."

"Open it," Shanon urged.

Carefully Max undid the ribbon and opened the box. Inside was a beautiful red-orange rose—and a card. Breathing in the delicate aroma of the rose, Max grinned. She picked up the small white envelope and pulled out the card. " 'A beautiful rose for a rose of a beauty. From PG.' Shanon, can you believe he sent me a flower?"

"Oh, Max, I'm so jealous. It's lovely and it's sort of your hair color. It smells great."

"Oh, Shanon, I'm scared. What if I do something really dumb tonight? What if he asks me to dance and I trip him and he breaks his nose. Or maybe he'll expect me to talk to him."

"Maxie, don't worry. He's met you before and obviously likes you. You'll be fine. Let's put your flower in water." Shanon filled up one of her empty soda bottles with water and Maxie placed the rose in it. She stood back and just grinned at it. "Come on, Cinderella, let's get dressed or else you'll never make it to the ball," Shanon teased. Walking to the closet, Shanon took off her bathrobe. She put on her new red skirt and a black sweater. "How do I look?"

"Very cool. I can't go. I'm going to look awful!" Maxie practically wailed, sitting down hard on her bed.

"Maxie, you're going and that's final. Now, put on the outfit Palmer picked out."

"Yes, sir," Maxie groaned. Reluctantly she pulled out her long, red plaid skirt and a green sweater.

"That looks so wonderful with your red hair," Shanon said as she combed her hair one more time.

"You think so?"

100

"Yes," Shanon assured her. "Now those green boots I love so much."

"Thanks, Shanon," Max said. Impulsively she jumped up and gave her roommate a hug. "You've been great about this—listening to me and encouraging me. Now, all you have to do is promise you'll be around in case I need you."

"Of course I will."

"And—"

"There's more?" Shanon exclaimed.

"Help me untangle my shoelaces?" Shanon laughed and knelt down at Max's feet. Feeling good inside, Maxie stared out the bedroom window. Suddenly she realized what she was looking at.

She jumped up, practically knocking Shanon over, and raced to the window. Gasping, she pressed her face right up against the glass. "Shanon, turn off the light," she exclaimed.

"What is it?"

"Just turn it off and come to the window! It's started to snow!"

Shanon shut the light off and joined Max at the window. In the darkened room, both girls could see the snow coming down hard.

"We've got to tell Dan and Maggie," Shanon insisted. "It's too dangerous to be riding a bike in this weather. It would be scary even if it were daylight."

"We'll get into trouble and Amy will really be punished."

"But I think it's worth it. We have to—we're talking about her safety."

"I think we should wait like we told Amy we would."

"But, Max . . ."

"Look, it's eight-thirty now. She has to be either at the diner or on her way back, right?"

"Yeah," Shanon answered uncertainly.

"So if she's in the diner, she's safe; and if she's on her way back, I'm sure she'll either come back slowly or stay where she is until it stops snowing."

"I hope you're right."

"We promised her, Shanon."

"I know. All right, we won't say or do anything until nine o'clock."

"Nine-thirty."

"Nine-fifteen."

"Done." Max glanced out the window again, her face looking troubled. "I hope we're doing the right thing," she murmured under her breath.

"Come on, I'll finish doing your shoelaces," Shanon said, forcing herself to look away from the window. Max sat down on her bed and Shanon knelt next to her sitting roommate and swiftly undid the knots. As she finished the last one, there was a light knock on their door. "Come in."

Palmer hesitantly opened the door. She stepped in the rest of the way. Already dressed in her black dress with the red bow and her red shoes, she looked perfect. She had one hand behind her back.

"Hi."

"Hi, Palmer. You look great! You ready?" Shanon asked.

"Yeah. I was wondering if it was okay if I walked with you to the dance."

"Of course."

"I mean, I didn't know if you both decided not to talk to me also."

"Palmer!" Shanon exclaimed, standing up. "I don't think what you did was right, and I think you should keep on apologizing until Amy accepts, but I know you won't. And Amy won't accept it anyway. No matter what though, you are still my friend."

"Mine, too," Maxie said as she stood up. "Shanon and I discussed it and we both agreed—we don't want to take sides."

"And we want you and Amy to be friends again," Shanon added. "But until then, we are both your friend and Amy's."

"We just hope you don't make it too difficult on the two of us."

"Thanks." Palmer stood there for a moment and then brought her hidden hand around to the front. In it she held two red envelopes. "Here. I decided that I wasn't going to send one to Sam, since he doesn't believe in them and it was pretty obvious that he wasn't going to send me one. But I wanted to send valentines to my friends."

"Thanks, Palmer," Shanon said immediately, hugging her. "I got one from my mother, but that doesn't count."

"Thanks," Maxie said, ripping hers open. "I love it!" She immediately put it up on her dresser.

"I had one for Amy, but since we're not talking since she's decided to be pigheaded about all of this—"

"Palmer!" Maxie warned, putting her hands on her hips.

"No badmouthing the other one!" Shanon reminded her.

"Okay, okay. I just wanted you to remember that not

talking to each other is her idea, not mine."

"We know," both girls said at the same time.

"Let's go."

"Where's Amy?" Palmer asked as she put on her down coat.

Maxie quickly glanced at Shanon and answered in a muffled voice as she put on her blue-gray cape. "She decided not to come to the dance. I don't know where she decided to hang out."

"Let's go," Shanon urged, carrying her coat and turning off the light in the bedroom. The three girls went down the stairs and toward the front door. Palmer peered out and shivered.

"It's really snowing out there. I think it's coming down harder."

"Don't say that!" Shanon exclaimed.

"Shanon, maybe you're right," Maxie said under her breath.

"Right about what?" Palmer asked, pulling on her red leather gloves.

"Nothing. Should we? There's Dan." Shanon pointed toward their English teacher who was looking out the dorm window. Noticing the girls, he waved at them, motioning them to come over.

"How are the famous Foxes?" he asked, buttoning up his coat. "Oops, we're missing someone. Where's Amy?"

Shanon grabbed Max's hand and both girls just stared at their teacher, unable to say a word. They looked at each other and then back at Mr. Griffith.

"Uh—she's—" Shanon tried to say, but no words would come out.

"You see, Mr. Griffith, uh—" Maxie began.

"Oh, there she is," he said, pointing behind the three girls. Eyes wide open, Max and Shanon slowly turned around and saw Amy walking toward them.

"Hi, Mr. Griffith," Amy said breezily, "lovely weather we're having."

"Yup. I was just asking your pals where you were. They seemed a little stunned by the question."

"It's sometimes hard to think on a Saturday," Amy joked.

"Are you ready to go to the dance? Maggie needed more time to get ready, so if you don't mind me tagging along with the four of you?"

Amy finally seemed speechless. She looked down at what she was wearing—black jeans, hiking boots, and a down jacket. "Uh, Mr. Griffith, why don't you go ahead with the others? I forgot something from upstairs. I'll meet you all there."

"Yeah, me, too. See you there, Mr. Griffith," Maxie added.

"Gosh, what a coincidence. I seem to need more tissues," Shanon said, digging into her purse.

"How about you, Palmer? Do you need to run up to the suite, too?"

"No, I'm ready to go now," Palmer said, putting her hand on Mr. Griffith's arm. "If you'll just help me over the icy patches . . ."

"I'd be charmed. See you ladies over there," Mr. Griffith called back as he and Palmer went outside.

"Amy, where have you been?" Maxie hissed as soon as she was sure Mr. Griffith was gone.

Amy grinned sheepishly. "I've been in the library for the past hour and a half."

"Amy!" Shanon practically exploded. "We've been worried sick, trying to decide what to do. To tell Dan and Maggie that you might be hurt somewhere out in the snow or not to tell them, petrified that you were hurt out in the snow."

"I'm sorry. I just couldn't come right back up. I had to think for a while by myself."

"Well, did you see him?" Maxie asked.

"Come upstairs with me while I change and I'll tell you." The three girls ran up the stairs and unlocked the suite door. As Amy washed and dressed, she told them her story. "Actually, I was only on the drive and it was freezing out there. And scary. I realized that I was crazy, biking out there at night. I might miss the gig tonight, but at least I'd be alive. He probably has another singer tonight anyway. I'll get a pass and go see him during the week. Anyway, I just didn't feel like coming back to the suite, so I went to the library and just sat by myself for a while. I hadn't planned on going to the dance, but I'd better—just to make sure Dan doesn't get too suspicious."

Like Palmer, Amy was dressed in black, but that was the only similarity. Instead of a sophisticated dress, she was wearing black leggings, a short black skirt, and a black midriff sweater. "A midriff in February?" Maxie asked.

"Gotta fight those February blues, you know! Besides, after a couple of dances, you'll wish you had a midriff on! Ready?"

"Yeah. Let's go."

Once they were outside, Shanon turned to Amy. "What are you going to say to Emmett?"

"That I want to play music with him. He's really good,

106

and I like him. I can't let this whole thing drop. It's too important to me, and he's too important to me."

"Do you like Emmett?"

"Nooo, not romantically. I've told both of you that a thousand times. At least," Amy said slowly, "I don't think it's romantic. But I definitely want to see him again and talk music and perform with him. He's good, Shanon, even if he is a 'creep,' to quote Palmer. Even Sam admitted that he's a good musician."

"But what about John?" Maxie asked.

"Wanting to see Emmett has nothing to do with John. I still want to write to him, I guess, but if he isn't at the dance, it won't kill me. He may not show up since I didn't invite him."

"But don't you want to see him?" Shanon crossed her fingers behind her back. She wanted the "old" Amy. The old Amy would be really excited to see her pen pal.

"It would be nice, but I'm not dying to see him. I haven't really missed writing to him, I don't think. I've been so busy with other things."

"Don't you think he misses you?" Shanon hinted.

"I don't know. We're just friends, you know."

"I would be so upset if Mars didn't show up. It's all I've been looking forward to for weeks," Shanon added.

"Well, I'm ready to rock and roll and have a great time!" Amy declared, taking a deep breath of the fresh air.

"It's not going to be the Heartbreak with the fabulous singer Amy Ho, but it will certainly be fun," Shanon agreed.

"Are you ready to meet Mr. Grant?" Amy asked, punching Max lightly on the arm.

"Maybe he won't be there."

"He'll be there or he'll have the Foxes to answer to!" Amy exclaimed. "Come on, you guys, let's run. I bet this rock star can still beat you to the dining hall!" Amy took off, with Max and Shanon, laughing, following close behind.

CHAPTER SEVENTEEN

When the three girls entered the decorated dining room, Shanon declared, "It's beautiful!" Maxie and Amy nodded wordlessly.

The room looked absolutely elegant. The regular tables were against the wall, but they were covered with red tablecloths. There were tall white candles and vases of flowers on each table. The girls could see the streamers and hearts that they had put up, but in the candlelight they created shadows and gave the room an air of mystery.

"I'm glad I changed out of my hiking boots," Amy said, giggling.

"It's my lady fair," a voice said behind them.

They turned around and Shanon exclaimed, "Mars!" He smiled and bowed. He was dressed in jeans, but had on a tux jacket and a red bow tie.

"A flower for you." He held up a deep red rose.

"Oh, Mars, it's beautiful!"

"Why don't you two go off and dance or something," Amy said with a laugh, giving Shanon a little push.

"See you later," Mars said as he took Shanon by the

hand. "You look great. It's just so great to see you. The room is great. Everything is great tonight!" He gave her a little hug and then stepped back.

Relieved that the lights were dim in the room so he couldn't see her blush, Shanon said, "You've changed. You really have muscles now."

"You noticed! Yeah, these workouts are really cool. Do you like it?" he asked shyly.

"I think you look wonderful, Mars. And I love the flower."

"I'm glad. Do you want to get something to drink?"

"That would be good. Isn't that Paul Grant?" Shanon pointed at someone who looked as if he were hiding behind one of the columns.

"Yeah, I guess he's being shy or something," Mars said quickly. "Let's go."

As they walked toward one of the refreshment tables, Shanon noticed Sam and Palmer dancing. Palmer was smiling and holding Sam's hands as they rocked to the music. Shanon waved and Palmer nodded, grinning.

"Who are you smiling at?" Sam asked.

"It's Shanon. She's at the drinks table with Mars."

"I didn't get a chance to ask you. Did everything go all right with Amy when you told her about Emmett?"

"Yes, everything's fine," Palmer answered, not looking at Sam.

"Palmer, let's go over to that corner for a moment," Sam said, pulling her off the dance floor. "I have something for you."

"What?" she asked, clapping her hands together.

He pulled a small white box out of his jacket pocket and handed it to her. Opening it quickly, Palmer gasped when she saw what was inside. It was a tiny heart locket.

"Oh, help me put it on, Sam," Palmer said, her eyes shining. "It's so lovely." She took it out of the box and gave it to Sam, who placed it around her neck and closed the clasp. "I love it."

"More than a valentine card?" he asked, laughing.

"I guess I was pretty obvious," Palmer admitted, touching the locket.

"Well, yes. I just couldn't find a card that was right. But the locket is . . . well, I hope you like it."

Smiling and taking his hand in hers, Palmer led him back out to the dance floor, for the deejay was playing a slow tune. They danced together easily, looking only at each other.

"I guess Palmer's happy," Maxie said to Amy, standing off to the side of the dancing.

"Yeah. Why don't you look for Paul and go dance with him?"

"Why don't you look for John?" Maxie retorted.

"I guess we're both avoiding guys. Is it that obvious?"

Maxie chuckled. "I think all four of us are avoiding each other. I keep noticing John and Paul skirting around wherever we're standing. If it didn't make me feel so horrible, it would be funny."

Amy faced her suitemate. "Let's make a deal. You go after Paul and I'll go find John. Then we'll both know how things stand, okay?"

"Good luck. Should you fail in your mission—"

"We're not going to fail. There's no such word as *failure* in the Fox vocabulary. I see John—wish me luck."

"Luck."

"Luck to you, Maxie." Amy gave her a thumbs-up and

went straight over to John, who was standing near the food table. "Hi, John."

He turned around, smiling, but he quickly stopped when he saw who it was. "Hello, Amy."

"How have you been?" she asked, shrugging a bit and crossing her arms in front of her.

"Fine. Thank you."

"Would you like to dance?"

"I don't think so."

"Oh." Amy looked down at the floor and off to the side before she could make herself look at him again. "You're really angry at me."

He put down the plate of food he was holding and then said, "Angry and hurt. I thought we were friends, but I guess not. Or at least not in the way I wanted us to be. I'm only a friend when you have the time and inclination, it seems. That's not good enough for me."

"There you are, John. Oh, hi, Amy," Georgette said as she walked up to them.

"Hi, Georgette."

"Uh, you ready for that dance, John?"

"Yes. See you, Amy." John took Georgette's hand and together they went out onto the dance floor.

"See you, John," Amy said as she picked up a celery stick and crunched down on it. She saw Maxie watching her, so she raised her celery stick and pointed it at Paul and then back at Max.

Maxie sighed and then walked over to the column that Paul was leaning against. "Hi, Paul."

He stood up straight, as if he were startled. "Hi, Maxie."

She waited for him to say something more, but he just stood there. "Uh, do you want to dance?"

"Let's wait for a faster one, okay? I'm not very good at slow dances."

"Oh, sure, that sounds good." Maxie groaned to herself, *How could I have asked him for a slow dance? What a numbskull!* "Thanks for the card, Paul. I really liked it."

"What card?"

"You know, the valentine card that you sent me."

"I didn't send you one."

"Yes, the blank with your own message in it and then signed P.G."

"Maxie, I'm not lying. I didn't send you any card, I'm sorry. Come on, let's dance. This is a great tune."

Max followed him, confused and hurt. If he didn't send it, who did? And if he did, why is he denying it?

As they danced, Maxie asked, "What about the rose today?"

Paul looked at her as if she were crazy. "Rose? I didn't send you a rose."

"But—oops, I'm sorry," Maxie apologized as she stepped on his foot.

"It's okay. You got one with a message and it was signed P.G.?" Maxie nodded and Paul burst out laughing.

"Forget this. I don't need to be laughed at," Maxie declared, walking off the floor. Paul grabbed her arm to stop her.

"No, Max, don't go. I'm sorry for laughing. Let me explain."

"What?" She stood there, glaring, her weight on one hip and her arms across her chest.

"Please, start dancing again. They're watching."

She started to dance as she looked around. "Who's watching?"

113

"Oh, sorry, was that your foot? Them. Mars and John." He nodded in two directions and Max looked. When she caught John's eyes, he looked away quickly. Mars did the same thing. "You see. I bet they sent those things and signed my name."

"This is so humiliating," Maxie groaned. "I'm sorry."

"No, I'm sorry," Paul said. "I'm sorry they've been doing this to you. Please don't stop dancing with me. If you do, they'll just do something else to get us talking and it might be worse than a card and a flower," he teased. "Besides, I've been wanting to dance with you, but I didn't think you would want to."

"I don't know. I just feel like such a dope!"

"Come on. We just danced for two minutes without either of us stepping on the other one. We're practically ready for MTV! Let's dance the next one."

Maxie laughed. "All right, but I just feel terrible that everyone is always pushing me on you."

"I don't mind." Paul tried to spin her, but he lost control and Maxie bumped into the next couple. "Sorry," Paul said to the couple. "You know, Maxie . . ."

"What?" she asked, realizing that she was having a great time.

"I'm real sorry now that I didn't send you the card and rose. Maybe I should thank them."

"Maybe we both should," she answered, smiling at him as he spun her around perfectly.

CHAPTER EIGHTEEN

Dear Sam,

This Valentine's Day will stand out as the best one I've ever had. Thank you so much for the locket; it's beautiful. I wear it all the time. You're right, the locket is much more romantic than a card.

I wish we could have Valentine dances every night, but that would be too perfect.

Can't wait to see you again,
Palmer

Dear Jose,

I hope your Valentine's Day was as much fun as mine. I hope that Hilary liked her valentine.

Just to let you know, I do not hate boys. I met my valentine and he's a great guy, although it turns out that he didn't send me the flower or the card. I had a nice time at the dance with him. His name is Paul Grant and he lives in the suite with Mars, John, and Rob. He's very nice—you would like each other. And he only stepped on my feet a few times, but I got him back by stepping on him, by accident of course.

Hope to see you soon.

Love,
Maxie

Dear Emmett,

I tried to come see you at Lulu's, but because of the snow I couldn't get there. I just want you to know that Palmer did not tell you the truth when she said I never wanted to see you again. She did that on her own and it's not true.

I would love to meet with you and play music with you. I still want to be in your band.

I hope to see you soon and I hope your gig was a huge success.

Best,
Amy Ho

Dear Amy,

I've thought about writing this letter for quite a while, but after seeing you at the dance I made up my mind to send this to you.

I don't think we should be pen pals anymore. Our friendship doesn't seem to be going anywhere and you don't seem to be very interested. You haven't written to me in weeks and then at the dance you acted as if everything was just normal. Well, it's not. You don't seem to be interested in anything I do, so instead of bothering you with letters, I'll just stop.

John Adams

116

Dear Mars,

I had the greatest time on Saturday night. Dancing with you is an experience! I loved it!

Maxie is still real angry at The Unknown. And she almost included me, too. Luckily she believed me that I knew nothing about it. I can't believe that you sent that card and flower in Paul's name.

She's not angry at Paul, which is good. And I know she had a great time at the dance. So even if your plan was underhanded, it still worked.

I just have one question—why do these Alma/Ardsley things happen so infrequently?

I want to see you soon.

Waiting impatiently,
Shanon

P.S. You looked great. I could definitely tell that you've been working out. But I thought you looked fine before the new you.

Dear Lisa,

I have some good news and some bad news. I'll get the good news out of the way first.

I got back my Lord of the Flies paper and got an A. Mr. Griffith said it was very imaginative. I wrote a long story (very short novel?) on what it would be like if all girls got stuck on an island. (Can you imagine all of Alma Stephens?) The best part was having Mr. Griffith trust me enough to give me two extensions so I could write my paper my way.

The other good news is that I had a great time at the

117

Valentine's Day Dance. Mars and I get along so well. And he bought me a beautiful red, red rose that I still have.

Amy did talk to Professor Bernard and they straightened everything out. He said that teenagers all have their moments. None of us quite understands what he means, but Amy's glad to be back with him, practicing and everything. Now she sings rock songs with him.

The bad news—and I even hate to write about it because it's so bad and writing it makes it true.

Palmer and Amy aren't talking anymore. They had a big blowup, and Amy just won't forgive Palmer. The suite just feels awful.

And John doesn't want to write to Amy anymore because he says that she doesn't seem interested enough in him and that the friendship isn't going anywhere.

I'm really upset. I want everything to be nice, the way it was, and happy. I mean it's okay if Amy and John don't become a couple, you know, but Amy doesn't seem to mind at all that she won't have a pen pal. Having pen pals is what made us the Foxes of the Third Dimension.

Lisa, what are we going to do? Everything is changing and different. I don't know if I can stand it. What's going to happen if Amy really gets hooked up with Emmett? What will happen if Palmer or Amy moves out of the suite? What happens if the other Unknowns decide that they don't want the rest of us as pen pals or friends?

Most importantly, what's going to happen to the Foxes of the Third Dimension? I wish I knew. I miss you!

Love,
Shanon

PEN PALS

Something to write home about . . .
another new Pen Pals story!

In Book 16, BOY CRAZY, everybody in Suite 3-D is acting weird! Palmer and Amy are barely speaking to each other. Palmer is spending more and more time with her new snobby friends. Shanon is holding the suite together singlehandedly—and it's not easy, the way Palmer's been acting! She's back to her old sneaky ways. An adorable Ardie named Paul Grant wants Max to be his pen pal— and Max isn't sure if she's interested. But when Palmer hears how rich Paul is, *she's* definitely interested!

P.S. Have you missed any Pen Pals? Catch up now!

PEN PALS #1: BOYS WANTED!

Lisa, Shanon, Amy, and Palmer advertise for boy pen pals.

PEN PALS #2: TOO CUTE FOR WORDS

Palmer decides she wants Amy's pen pal instead of her own.

PEN PALS #3: P.S. FORGET IT!

Palmer will do anything to prove that her pen pal is better than Lisa's.

PEN PALS #4: NO CREEPS NEED APPLY

Palmer realizes that winning a tennis match could mean losing her pen pal.

PEN PALS #5: SAM THE SHAM

Palmer's new pen pal seems too good to be true—and he is.

PEN PALS #6: AMY'S SONG

Amy, Palmer, Shanon, and Lisa go on a class trip to London.

PEN PALS #7: HANDLE WITH CARE

Shanon runs for student council president—against Lisa.

PEN PALS #8: SEALED WITH A KISS

Amy stars in a rock musical with Lisa's pen pal Rob.

PEN PALS #9: STOLEN PEN PALS

Four girls from a rival school try to steal the Foxes' pen pals.

PEN PALS #10: PALMER AT YOUR SERVICE

When her parents cut her allowance, Palmer has to take a waitress job.

PEN PALS #11: ROOMMATE TROUBLE

Lisa thinks Shanon's new friend Lorraine is taking advantage of her.

PEN PALS #12: LISA'S SECRET

Lisa is afraid her parents are getting a divorce.

PEN PALS #13: LISA, WE MISS YOU

Amy, Shanon, and Palmer get a new suitemate named Maxine Schloss.

PEN PALS #14: THE MYSTERY ABOUT MAXIE

Maxie has a mysterious pen pal.

PEN PALS SUPER SPECIAL #1: DREAM HOLIDAY

Palmer, Amy, and Shanon go to Maxie's New York townhouse for the Christmas party of their dreams!

BIG NEWS!
GET YOUR NAME
IN A PEN PALS BOOK!

Everybody's getting into PEN PALS—reading PEN PALS books
. . . writing to their own pen pals—and now there's even a way
to get your name in a Pen Pals book.

Every month, the author of PEN PALS, Sharon Dennis Wyeth
is going to name a character in a PEN PALS book after a PEN
PALS reader. In PEN PALS #10, PALMER AT YOUR SERVICE,
there's a character named Megan who was named after a PEN
PALS reader. Maybe you'll be next.

All you have to do is write to PEN PALS headquarters. Tell us
about yourself and your pen pal. Tell us what you and your pen
pal do to keep in touch, to share your feelings or just for laughs.
We'll share some of the PEN PALS news and print the names
of pen pals who send us letters right in the next PEN PALS
book. And—we'll pick one person each month for the special
honor of having a character named for him or her.

So get out your pens and start writing! Send your letters to:

PEN PALS HEADQUARTERS
c/o PARACHUTE PRESS
156 FIFTH AVE. ROOM 325
NEW YORK, NY 10010

Letters will be judged on originality and content.

IF YOU DON'T HAVE A PEN PAL, FILL OUT THE FORM ON THE NEXT PAGE AND
GET ONE!

WANTED: BOYS — AND GIRLS —
WHO CAN WRITE !

Join the Pen Pals Exchange and get a pen pal of your own!

Fill out the form below.

Send it with a self-addressed stamped envelope to:

PEN PALS EXCHANGE
c/o The Trumpet Club
PO Box 632
Holmes, PA 19043
U.S.A.

In a couple of weeks you'll receive the name and address of someone who wants to be your pen pal.

here